SUGAR COOKIE *Kisses*

CHERRY LAKE FIREFIGHTERS - BOOK 1

KATIE O'CONNOR

SNARKY HEART PRESS

– Sugar Cookie Kisses –
– Cherry Lake Fire Fighters Book 1 –

Published October 2023
(katieohwrites.com)

ISBN: 978-1-989816-74-5 Digital Edition
ISBN: 978-1-989816-75-2 Print Edition

Design and cover art by Mad Cat Design
Editing by Terri St. Clair

Dedication

To all the volunteers out there.
Your quiet service does not go unnoticed.
And
To the ladies of the *Sweet and Swoony Holiday Box Set* in
which this story first appeared. Thanks for having me along.

About this Book

When dedicated receptionist and volunteer Sage Taylor is looking for help with the Christmas holiday toy drive, she seeks the assistance of the local fire hall. She isn't expecting to be saddled with the entirely too attractive, Brad Putnam. He may be cute, but his Christmas spirit is lacking. She'll have to make do. After all, kids love firemen, even taciturn ones. Watching Brad's attitude soften might just steal her heart.

Fire fighter Brad Putnam isn't one for helping out. He'd rather stay in the fire hall, out of the public's eye, and hold down the fort. When his boss assigns him to a charity drive, he's annoyed. Much to his surprise, Sage Taylor is lovely, and her generous heart draws him in almost as much as the grateful smiles of their gift recipients. He finds he'll do anything to make Sage happy. He may even give up his Grinch persona.

Christmas, it seems, is a time of giving, and if Brad and Sage aren't careful, they might just give each other their hearts.

Chapter One

"Do you really think the fire hall is the best place to get volunteers?" Sage scraped a hand through her shoulder length blonde hair and gave her boss a quizzical look. "I was thinking more along the lines of nurses from the hospital."

Firemen were big, burly, and too enticing for her peace of mind. Nurses were calm, quiet, and reassuring.

"The nurses are too busy," her boss said. "The boys at the hall have more free time. We've used them before. Cherry Lake doesn't have many fires. Those boys are sitting around waiting for something to do. Wander over and ask the chief if they can assist us again this year." Dr. Ingram went into his office and closed the door behind him. By us, he meant her.

"I guess that ends the discussion." She'd only been in this job for six months and she'd learned that her late thirties boss rarely changed his mind. He was a fabulous doctor, kind and understanding with their patients. What he lacked was social skills. He was pretty reclusive. Which made the clinic running the toy drive every year something of a puzzle to Sage. She shrugged it didn't really matter. The task was hers, so she'd take it on full throttle.

She had no issues with heading the Christmas toy drive. In fact, she couldn't wait to get started, but she'd been hoping for assistants who were less...manly than firefighters. The only female on the squad was out with a broken femur, and would be no help beyond record keeping.

Sage packed her lunch bag into her backpack and locked up. Dr. Ingram always stayed late to finish his charting. "Off to the fire hall," she muttered to herself. She might as well stop on the way home; she was passing right by.

Bundled up against the November air, she hurried down the block, her breath crystalizing in the icy cold. She ignored the pretty flakes falling from the sky. She was a woman on a mission. Get help with the drive, get home, get a dinner, and unwind. The clinic had been bustling with patients today. There was an intestinal bug running through the elementary school. As much as she loved her job, it was a relief to get out of there. Pinch hitting for the nurse wasn't her idea of fun.

Like the clinic, the fire hall sat on Main Street, just down from the retail shops. She waved at a crew of civic employees who were busy taking down Halloween decorations and replacing them with snowflakes and candy canes. Halloween stayed up for a week or two after the big day and then began its slow transformation to Christmas. By the last week of November, Cherry Lake would be a holiday paradise.

One thing her new hometown did was go all out for the holidays. The Halloween weekend events had brought hundreds, maybe a thousand tourists to their sleepy town, and she adored the way her friends and neighbors threw themselves into every event. Civic pride was one of the things she adored about Cherry Lake.

The firehall was a large red brick building with white trim. All three bay doors were closed, though there were lights on inside and someone was busy stringing multicolored lights around the inside of the front window.

She paused at the end of the walkway to watch him. She'd met a lot of the fire fighters, but this man was unfamiliar to her and he was good looking. Very good looking. Maybe drool-worthy. He wasn't overly tall, but he had thick dark hair and broad shoulders. Man, she did love broad shoulders. Other women went for height, not Sage, she loved a solid chest. The man looked up once or twice with a puzzled expression. After a few glances, he disappeared from view. Ten seconds later, the front door opened.

"Hey there. Are you okay?" He strode toward her, a concerned frown etched on his handsome face.

She swallowed hard and attempted to keep a blush from heating her face.

"Miss? Are you okay?" He scowled down at her, his expression somewhere between frustration and concern. Snowflakes drifted around him and his blue eyes squinted at her. Somewhere nearby she heard *Hark the Herald Angels Sing* playing softly.

"Miss? Are you okay?"

"What?" She realized she'd zoned out for a second. "Yeah. I'm fine." She shook her head to clear away the cobwebs of her over-active imagination. The street was silent, the snow dampening all sound. There was no music. She'd imagined it. Weird. "You caught me daydreaming."

"Oh yeah" He winked. "About what?" There was a flirty quality to his voice that went straight to her feminine ego, though she doubted he was serious.

"The holidays, of course. It's the time for good cheer and generosity. Is Chief Ramirez in? I'm here to see him." She forced herself to look away from his lovely blue eyes.

"Sure. Let me help you inside. Watch the snow." He took her elbow and gently led her to the station's front door.

She was so astounded by the chivalrous action she didn't think to protest. The sidewalk and driveway only had a skiff of snow and as they approached the building, a bulky man in a blue parka came out and started sweeping the fluff away.

"Come in." Her guide paused to wipe his boots.

She wiped hers and unwound her scarf. She pulled off her wool hat and stuffed it into her pocket before unbuttoning her coat. His gaze followed her actions. His interest was somewhere between unnerving and titillating.

The fire hall was quiet. In the distance she heard a television and deep male laughter. The sounds were comforting, like all was right with the world.

She thrust her hand at her guide. "Hi. I'm Sage Taylor. I work in Dr. Ingram's clinic."

They clasped hands and a wave of warmed washed up her arm. *Probably just because he was warm and she was chilled from being outside. Yeah, that was it.*

"Nice to meet you, Sage. Brad Putnam. Come on, I'll take you to the chief," he said briskly and waved for her to follow him.

She tried not to ogle his backside as he walked away, but even in his relaxed fit uniform trousers, it was taut and enticing. His hips were lean, his back strong, and his shoulders broad. Pure masculine perfection. She blinked away the attraction before he caught her drooling. It wasn't that she wasn't interested. She was. But she didn't want a man in such a dangerous position. He could get hurt at any time. Give her a nice safe dentist, or maybe an accountant.

Brad rapped on an open office door. "Chief Ramirez, there's someone from the clinic here to see you."

The chief looked up from behind his battered wood desk. Oak unless she missed her guess, and it matched the framed pictures of his family that hung from all the walls. The photos were intermingled with awards for his service.

"Sage, come in. What can I do for you today? Come in. Sit down. Putnam, get our guest something warm to drink. What can we get you, Sage? Coffee? We have a tasty eggnog hot cocoa."

"No, thanks." She tried not to sound dubious about the weird combination of tastes.

"It's better than it sounds," Brad put in from the doorway. "It was my mother's secret family recipe. I don't share with just anyone."

She perched on the edge of a chair across from the chief and glanced back at Brad. His brows pinched together and there was something sad in his voice that prompted her to accept the beverage. "I guess, since it's so special. I will have one. Thank you." She turned away before she got caught up in his mesmerizing blue eyes.

"You've got it."

She explained her mission to the chief. "Dr. Ingram says your crew helps out every year. This year we're collecting for the hospital as well as for a couple dozen less fortunate families. We just want everyone to have a wonderful Christmas."

"Is it just toys this year?" he asked.

"Not at all. We're doing clothing, toys, school supplies, anything really. There's another group doing food, and one doing outerwear. I'm sure there will be crossover. The heads of the groups will meet once a week to exchange information. The back room of the clinic is full of boxes waiting to be delivered to stores so people know where to drop items off. We just need to assemble and wrap them."

"I'll have one of the guys pick them up. We can wrap them up for you. The last few months have been blessedly quiet. Although now that the snow has arrived, that's likely to change." His eyes were sadly thoughtful. He visibly shook off the morose expression.

They discussed her needs over the coming weeks. A soft step behind her alerted her to Brad's return.

"Ah, Putnam, just the man we needed." The chief grinned.

Brad frowned.

No! Not him. His mood had fluctuated too much in the few minutes they'd been together. The kids need a cheerful, level-headed person. She bit her lip to keep from blurting her dismay. "I'm happy for any help I can get," she said graciously despite her inner turmoil.

"What can I do, chief?" His voice was wary as he set two steaming mugs on the desk. Each was topped with whipped cream and a light sprinkling of nutmeg. Chocolate and cinnamon swirled on the air. Despite herself, she was eager to try the tempting treat. Who could resist whipped cream?

"Oh, it smells delicious," she exclaimed. "Thank you."

The chief made a show of checking a list he pulled from his desk drawer. "Putnam, it's your turn on the charity roster. You'll be helping Sage with the holiday toy drive. You're at her beck and call until it's finished. Consider yourself off duty unless there's a fire or major accident. Give her as much time as she needs. This charity is near and dear to my heart."

Doc had told Sage that eight years ago, the chief's sister's family had been recipients of the toy and food drives. Rumor said the town's generosity with her plight was one of the reasons he settled in Cherry Lake.

"Are you sure you want *me*?" Brad asked, reluctance clear in his voice. He stuffed his hands in his pockets and stared at the floor.

"Absolutely!" The chief rubbed his hands together.

"But I don't know anything about kids or toys or charity," he grumbled.

"You know more than you think," the chief said and stood up, mug in hand. "Besides, Sage will show you what to do. I'll leave you two alone to iron out the details."

Brad scowled at her. She puffed out a breath and took a sip of the steaming drink to give her a moment to gather her thoughts. Aside from a quick smile and that one random wink, this guy had been grumpy. Almost surly. She'd prefer to work with someone with a little more holiday spirit. *But if he was who the chief chose, she'd work with him and keep him away from the kids. She'd find someone else to play Santa at the hospital.*

"Do you even like Christmas?" she asked at last. Worry knotted her stomach.

Katie O'Connor

Chapter Two

"I don't have anything against Christmas, if that's what you mean." Brad leaned against the doorjamb and looked at her. *What was her name again? Oh yeah, Sage.* The name suited her. She had an earthy, chill vibe. He could picture her doing yoga in a flower garden. Why he imagined that, he didn't know. He mentally shrugged.

Her silky blonde hair was accentuated by the emerald green sweater she wore over her utilitarian work pants. Her brown eyes snapped with fire.

"I meant, do you like Christmas and do you enjoy charity work?" Her brows squinched together giving her the look of a doubtful mother.

"I don't have a problem with either. I'm part of the station's snow shoveling program and I help mow lawns for seniors." *What was she driving at?*

"Are you going to be okay delivering gifts to children? You'll need to be cheerful and upbeat in some pretty sad circumstances. The holidays are hard for children with cancer and those stuck in the hospital. You'll have to dress up as Santa..." she trailed off as if daring him to back out of the task.

Well, he'd show her. He could make himself the cheeriest elf on the planet. He smirked. "Why, Miss Sage, I do believe you doubt my abilities?" he did his best Doc Holiday impression and almost laughed when she rolled her eyes. She had spunk.

"Why, Brad, I do believe you're funning with me," she threw his cheap movie reference back at him. "Come on, Brad, where's your Christmas spirit?"

He didn't need Christmas spirit. He wanted to tell her that as a bachelor with no immediate plans for a serious relationship and no family left alive, he wasn't particularly enamored with the holidays. He didn't dislike them, but he didn't celebrate them either. Holidays were when he racked up overtime so the rest of the crew could be with their families.

Instead of arguing about the beauty of holidays, he said, "I'll be the best danged Santa you've ever seen. Trust me." Her doubt annoyed him. How could someone with such a sunny smile and shining eyes make him feel so ... inadequate? "Christmas is for kids. I'm all in for giving them a great one."

She leaned back in her chair and sipped her cocoa. The flavor was smooth and complex. Nutmeg, cinnamon, chocolate, cream, and something she couldn't quite place. She toasted him with the mug. "This is wonderful. I'm glad I tried it." She looked him up and down, a slight frown turning down the corners of her luscious lips. Abruptly, she smiled. "You know what, I believe you will be a great Santa."

That lovely smile warmed him all the way to his toes. Maybe working with this spitfire wouldn't be all bad, which was a good thing, because he knew the chief wouldn't let him back out of it. He was stuck. He might as well make the best of it.

She smiled at him again, joy and excitement flashing in her eyes. She was lovely in her happiness. Yeah, this wasn't going to be bad at all. What man didn't like spending time with an attractive woman, and Sage ticked off a lot of his dating boxes. Not that they were dating.

Katie O'Connor

Chapter Three

When Sage pulled into the parking lot behind the clinic the next morning, Dr. Ingram's SUV wasn't there yet, but there was a large four by four truck idling two stalls down from her spot. A nervous shiver raced down her spine. Cherry Lake was a small town but that didn't make it immune to crime. She was about to back away when Brad jumped out, a big grin on his face, and a second man in uniform hopped out of the other side.

"Morning, Sage," Brad called. "We're here to pick up those boxes. Chief says we're to get them wrapped up for delivery. We'll store them at the station until drop off. Does that work for you?"

"Good morning." Gosh, his smile was devastatingly delicious. "Who's your friend?"

The man strode around the truck and offered his hand. "Gibson Baker, deputy chief. Sorry I missed your visit yesterday. Happy to be of service." He chuckled.

"Especially since it is dead at the station. Don't get me wrong, I don't want to be busy with fires, but after a while, waiting gets old."

"Nice to meet you and I'm thrilled to have extra help."

Brad frowned at her enthusiastic greeting. "Let's get this done."

Oh, he was grumpy this morning. So much for his eager arrival. "Come inside. I'll get you the boxes, but I don't have the wrapping paper yet. I'm expecting a shipment from a supplier this morning." She unlocked the back door and led them inside.

"Can I get either of you a coffee? It will only take a minute." She wasn't sure why she offered, maybe in thanks for the eager assistance.

"No, thanks," Brad said.

"I would love a coffee," Gibson declared with a smirk at Brad. Clearly there was some kind of dynamic or rivalry between the men.

She shucked off her coat and hung it on the coat rack and put her boots on the mat. "Don't worry about your boots. Come in." She padded, sock-footed, to the front of the clinic to find her shoes and flip on more lights. The motion light in the back hall didn't illuminate much. The men followed right behind her.

"It's a beautiful day," she declared. "The sun just lights up yesterday's snow like it's full of diamonds." Glittering snow was her favorite aside from big fluffy flakes that took an eternity to fall.

"Or sparkling fairy lights," Gibson said.

"It'll be slush in an hour," Brad grumped.

For a man who was so good looking with such an amazing smile, he sure had a sour attitude. She hoped the chief knew what he was doing when he assigned Brad to be her assistant. Maybe the chief was looking for a holiday miracle to fix that attitude. The idea had her grinning. She adored everything about Christmas, which made her just the person to give this grinch a taste of holiday magic. She almost rubbed her hands in glee.

"Right this way, gentlemen." She led them into the small staff area and flipped the switch on the coffee pot. She's set it to brew last night before she left. "Don't you just love the scent of coffee in the morning? Take a seat."

She slid a plate of sugar cookies in front of them. "Help yourself."

"How long have you been in Cherry Lake?" Gibson asked.

"Oh, just since spring. I wanted a change from where I grew up. I still wanted a small town, just not as small as where I came from. Fox Creek was great, but it's not much more than a blip on the road map."

"I have friends there. Cute little town. Are you married?" Gibson asked.

Brad growled almost inaudibly.

A blush heated her cheeks. It was flattering that he asked. Gibson was tall and lean, and very attractive but he didn't appeal to her the way Brad's broad shoulders did. Too bad Brad was a sour-puss. "I'm single." Something compelled her to add, "I'm much too busy to date right now. I think this toy drive will pretty much eat up all my spare time."

She turned her attention to the coffee pot. She slipped a mug under the filter to catch the drips and poured two other mugs while the pot sputtered to a finish. She carried those to the table and returned with the third one and a small carton of cream. She risked a glance at Brad, his scowl had ebbed to a tiny frown. Interesting. He had a very expressive face, even if the thoughts behind those expressions were hard to understand.

"What's your plan for the drive?" Brad asked.

"I'm going off Moira's notes. I don't know if you knew her. She was receptionist here before I was hired. She ran the drive for twenty years. She's retired and on a cruise with her husband. Can you imagine, a year-long cruise?" What a dream that would be.

"Moira was great," Brad said. "Very efficient, but still with a great bedside manner. Or rather, desk-side manner. It was only two years ago that Doc finally hired a nurse. Before he did, Moira stepped in when Doc needed help. Things have gotten busier since Cherry Lake started to grow, and having a nurse has been good for Doc."

"You'll do great in Moira's role. Renna mentioned how calm you were when she busted up her leg," Gibson said.

Sage winced. She'd been the first on the scene at an accident. Renna, a firefighter, had been in bad shape. Sage kept her company while they waited for help. They'd struck up a friendship. Renna was due to have her cast off any day now, though she wouldn't be back at work until she finished a long course of physio.

She decided to get the charity talk rolling. "I've got three dozen boxes to start. Once they're wrapped, I'll drop them off at schools, churches, and businesses. I'll work up a schedule for checking them. I think we want to empty them regularly."

"Maybe you should leave one of two items in each after collection," Brad said. "Make it look like people are giving, but encourage them to add their own donation. Some people will see a full bin and think their support isn't needed. Others might see an empty bin and think nobody supports the charity because it isn't worthy."

She stared at him, shocked by his insight. "That makes so much sense."

"You, we, could also put small trees in each location. We could put tags on them with the name and age of each child," Brad added.

"Great idea," she gushed. "They'd feel like they were buying for someone they know. You're brilliant."

Brad's smile was short lived but radiant. "I looked up ideas last night. If I have to help out with this, I want to give it my best shot."

"I really appreciate that." She patted his hand in gratitude. Heat raced up her arm and she jerked her hand back.

"Will we be emptying the bins, or replacing them?" Gibson asked.

"Replacing them makes more sense," Brad said. "Haul out the old and bring in the new. More efficient. If you have enough boxes, that is. Plus, I think the boxes might get worn, depending on the weight of the paper we cover them with."

"Then, we can reuse the boxes to deliver the gifts. It will make it extra festive to have wrapped boxes. An extra layer of Christmas joy," Gibson said.

They chatted back and forth on ideas for implementation of the drive. Every time Brad made a suggestion, Gibson added one. Her head pivoted back and forth between the two of them until she felt like she was at a tennis match. It was a relief when Dr. Ingram strolled in and busted up the discussion.

She had to open the clinic in two minutes. She'd gotten so wrapped up in the discussion she clean forgot about pulling the day's patient files. She'd have to hustle. Still, she didn't regret one second of the conversation.

Gibson was charming, and despite his constant flirting, she realized that he wasn't serious about dating her. Brad was a good guy, generous and thoughtful, even though he had a tendency toward grumpy. There was definitely something between the two men. It felt like a good-natured rivalry, with a bit of an edge. Their constant back and forth made her increasingly curious about her grumpy elf.

"What was that all about," Brad snapped at Gibson as he drove away from the clinic. "What's with all the flirting? She's a nice girl, too good for a playboy like you."

"Just testing the waters," Gibson gloated. "Sage is good looking, and did you notice how that slim skirt highlighted her backside?

Brad punched his friend in the shoulder. "Don't talk about her like that. She's a respectable woman."

And hot! He liked how she didn't berate him for being out of sorts, and how she praised him for his ideas. He'd gotten lucky when insomnia kept him up last night and he'd spent his time researching how to run a charity drive. It gave him ideas to input this morning.

"I think I'll ask her out." Gibson stared straight ahead like he hadn't dropped a bombshell.

"Back off, man."

"You don't date. Ever. What do you care?" He turned to stare at Brad.

"She's in a public position. She needs to be respectable, not associated with you." What was with Gibson being so dense all of a sudden?

"Are you implying that I'm not respectable? I am deputy chief of the station. In case you forgot."

"You're one step above a serial dater. Why all the women you go out with still respect you is beyond me. Leave this one alone." He drove slowly down the slushy street, careful not to splash any pedestrians.

"Whoa! Wait! Are you interested in the lovely Sage? Is that why you're warning me off? You want her for yourself!" Gibson crowed. "You moved back to town five years ago, and haven't dated once despite the women throwing themselves at you. What makes Sage so special that you'd stake a claim the day after you met her?"

They pulled around the fire hall and into the staff parking lot. He didn't bother to answer Gibson's question.

As they unloaded the boxes, Gibson said, "I'll give you until Valentine's Day, then she's fair game. Maybe it's time I settled down." He paused. "I like Sage. I like her a lot. She cute. She's civic minded. She's got a delectable body. She's intelligent. I won't let her waste away just because you're a coward, so consider yourself warned. She's safe from me. For now. The rest of the guys are a different story."

Brad groaned.

If he warned the other guys off, he'd be the brunt of months of teasing. If he didn't, any one of them might bump into Sage and ask her out. An idea hit him. Unless, as her number one elf, he was constantly at her side.

All he had to do was figure out how to help her, and stay on her good side. She was upbeat and cheerful and he didn't want to do anything to upset her. He wasn't super into Christmas, but that was more due to being single and alone than anything else. Being an only child had been great for years, but as his parents aged, then passed, he wished they'd given him a sibling. The guys at the station were amazing and they usually invited him to their celebrations. Last year, he'd had four Christmas dinners, but it wasn't the same. While they were family of sorts, they weren't *family*.

Katie O'Connor

Chapter Four

When Sage arrived at the fire hall, she expected it to be quiet, like on her first visit. She walked through the front door and was greeted by raucous laughter. She doubted anyone would hear if she called out. She wiped off her boots and walked inside.

The merriment came from down the hall, beyond the reception desk and the chief's office. She headed toward the noise and passed a door with a wide window. Through the window she saw the fire engines and two ambulances snug in their bays ready for a call out.

With each stride, the merriment got louder. She stepped through another doorway and stopped in shock. Eight were medics, others were fire fighters, and a few wore civilian clothing. The group surrounded a pair of with their men hands locked together, and elbows on the table. Arm wrestling. Typical men. Just like her brothers.

Cheers and jeers bounced off the walls with Chief Ramirez teasing along with everyone else. She recognized the man on the opposite side of the table as a medic, one of the ones who had come to Renna's aid when she broke her leg. The other combatant sat with his back to the door, shoulders tense and neck muscles bulging in concentration. He had a delicious set of broad shoulders. She recognized him instantly.

Brad.

Her heart did a little pitapat.

"Hi, guys," she addressed the room.

Everyone turned her way. The medic glanced up and Brad slammed the medic's arm down, winning the contest. Oops. She should have stayed quiet, though she didn't expect her voice to be heard above the teasing.

Brad and the medic shook hands amicably and he turned to look at her. "Sage. We're ready if you are."

"Brad, hi." She hoisted a container. "I brought cookies."

The men swarmed her. Once they were all munching, she waved her clipboard in the air. "I've broken the drop-offs into sections. I thought we could split up to distribute them." She'd been to the station the day before to inspect the boxes. She'd been surprised at how neatly they were wrapped, inside and out.

A small complement of firemen and medics needed to remain at the station in case of an emergency; the rest suited up for the task. With ten people working in pairs, they'd have the boxes dropped off in no time. She'd already been to Cherry Lake's two other firehalls and set those volunteers in motion. Chief Ramirez was in charge of all three stations.

After a bit of shuffling, everyone was gone except Sage and Brad. "I guess we're together," she said.

"Lucky me."

Unless she was mistaken, there was pleasure in his voice when he said "lucky me". She glanced up at him. He stood about five inches taller than her own five foot five. Just enough height to seem strong, manly, and yes, protective.

"We're hitting medical and dental clinics," she warned him. "Plus, we have a couple to drop off at the hospital. One for the lobby, and one for the Children's Ward." He frowned. "It's not going to be that bad."

She had mapped out the most efficient order for dropping the collection bins. Before she knew it, they were parking in the hospital lot.

"It feels weird to be collecting at the hospital where we'll be delivering some of the gifts," Brad said.

"Not really. According to Moira's notes, this is one of the best collection places. People feed bad because they're leaving and others must stay."

"Isn't that manipulative?"

She hadn't considered that aspect. "I guess. Maybe. But the beauty of gratitude is that it can flow downhill. Like when a lottery winner gives money to charity. This is the same idea. People grabbing something in the gift shop might just drop a toy or book into our bin. Last week, I had a call from a woman who was taking her newborn triplets home. She was so happy she wanted to donate to the other patients here. She gave me a large cash donation." She paused.

"I believe in the inherent generosity of most people. I'm counting on that to make this the best toy drive ever. That means dropping as many bins as we can. Besides, the gift shop requested a bin."

Brad was silent for so long she was certain he was manning a counter-argument. "I'm still a little leery, but if Moira said it works, who am I to argue. She used to run all the charity events. She's an organizational wizard. Let's do this."

He leaped out of his SUV and opened the back. He had the last three boxes out before she hit the pavement.

"Oh, we only need two," she said. "I must have miscalculated."

"Maybe so, but if we put the last on by the admin office, maybe we'll get some staff donations. Or maybe a couple vendors here for business might feel generous. Like you said, we need to believe in the generosity."

They locked up and went inside. Sage carried the boxes and tags while Brad carried the pre-lit trees to hold the tags. The tags were shaped like Christmas bulbs, trees, and angels. Each had a name and age neatly printed on the front and a list of gift ideas on the back. The names were made up but the ages were accurate and the gift ideas from children of the same age. The changed names were to protect those with distinctive names, like five-year-old leukemia patient Xavier.

They checked in with the office and set up the trees and boxes. It only took a few minutes and they were headed out.

"What's next on the agenda?" Brad asked.

"Not much. I'm headed to the church. We're setting up a sorting and wrapping area in the basement. I need to check on the progress."

"What is there to do? We just dropped off the bins." He sounded puzzled.

"There's a ton to do." She laughed at his naivety. "The church has been collecting all year. You'd be surprised how many unused toys are dropped in the charity bin for the Ladies Auxiliary resale shop. The church saves them for redistribution. In exchange, we give them the gently used toys we find in our bins."

The climbed into Brad's truck and he blasted the heater.

"But first," she said, "we have to set up the stations. Each one needs wrap, tags, scissors, tape. All the important things. Even bows. An anonymous donor gave us two thousand bows." She couldn't help but grin. Bows were a small thing, but would make the gifts extra special. "Toys are sorted by age, and in some cases gender. Each is wrapped, batteries added if needed, and tagged accordingly. Today is for getting the tables ready and maybe wrapping if I can."

"I had no idea a toy drive was this complex." He paused. "Don't you have to work?"

"Nope. Dr. Ingram hired a temp for December so I'd have enough time to get everything done. The temp is his donation, or rather I am. Just like you're the station's contribution."

"Take me to your wrapping," he quipped.

The church was unlocked and after a brief chat with the harried minister, they headed to the basement.

"Whoa. This place is huge," Brad exclaimed. His voice echoed in the cavernous space.

"Nothing is set up." She looked around in dismay. There were racks of tables and chairs at the far end and boxes of supplies near the door, but nothing was ready. "I thought they'd have the tables set up at least." Her spirits dropped to the floor. Was this how it was going to be? Promises made and then broken? She wondered what happened to prevent things from being ready. Perhaps whatever happened was the reason for the minister's distraction. She made a conscious decision to make the best of it. They could handle this.

"No tables? No problem," Brad declared as if reading her mind, "I've set up more than one table. Your wish is my command. Let's do this thing. Time's a wasting." He rubbed his hands together, dropped his jacket on the floor, and strode toward the tables. "Where do you want the first one?"

Her purse and jacket joined his and she raced after him, grinning at his eager enthusiasm. Now that was some Christmas spirit. "We'll need tables by age." She rattled of a list. "I want them in a ring with room behind them for boxes of wrapped items. We can store the unwrapped in the center."

"Okay. I've got the tables. You get the chairs." He hoisted a table and had it set up before she got the first chair down from the pile. The man was a powerhouse.

Chapter Five

The basement reminded Brad of someone's unfurnished living room. It was brightly lit with cream walls and pale gray carpet. Cheerful nature prints decorated the walls. An unlit tree towered in one corner and a foot-tall nativity scene rested on the carpet below its branches.

He surreptitiously watched Sage as he set out the tables. She moved briskly, wasting no motions. Her blonde hair fluttered as she moved. Her quick strides emphasized the length of her legs. She hummed *Frosty the Snowman* as she worked. Poetry in motion.

"I think we need music," he declared. He pulled out his phone and strode toward the podium at the end of the room. "I'll bet there's a sound system." He searched until he found a connection, selected a holiday play list, and started it.

Rocking Around the Christmas Tree poured out of speakers mounted on the wall. Sage danced the remaining chairs into place and stood in the center of the room. He was mesmerized by the slight motion of her hips, as if she couldn't help but dance.

He sidled up to her and offered his hand. "Care to dance?" He raised one eyebrow in question.

A brilliant smile lit her face. "Yes. Please." She clasped his hand and they did a slow jive around the open central space. She was light on her feet. Her laughter rang out, stealing his heart. She had so much joy in life that it bubbled out of her. They danced through three songs and when *Silent Night* came on, they stood staring at each other. The lyrics echoed the peace in his heart just being with Sage.

He wanted to keep dancing. She felt so wonderful in his arms. She smelled like the sugar cookies she'd brought to the station. Vanilla with a hint of cinnamon. He sighed. "Guess we better get back to work."

"I could use a coffee. There's pod pot in the kitchenette." She pointed to a door on the left. "Did you want a cup?"

"I'd love one. Cream and sugar in mine. I need energy."

"Dancing too much for you?" she teased.

"Late shift last night. One of the guys called in sick. Caught that bug going around the school."

"Oh no. I should get you back to the station. You need to rest." A worried frown turned down the corners of her mouth.

"I'm good. I'm used to lack of sleep. One of the hazards of the job. At least we didn't get a callout last night, so I did get a short nap in. The medics had a couple calls. Nothing serious," he added in case she was worried.

Coffee in hand they returned to the main room. "I was thinking we'd start by putting out supplies at each table. Wrapping paper first because the rolls are pretty big." She opened a box and pulled out a roll. It was about two feet long and eight inches deep.

"Holy cow," she exclaimed. "These are heavy."

"Industrial rolls?" He asked, taking it out of her hands.

She dug through the box and opened several more. "There are no stands! They were supposed to send stands with cutters. We paid for them."

Her dismay sliced through him. "Can you call them? Get them rush shipped?"

"I can try. I guess."

"If they can't get them out in time, I bet we could make some. A couple pieces of wood and some doweling. You'd have to cut by hand instead of tearing, but that wouldn't be a problem, would it? On a stand the rolls would roll well."

"That's better than trying to roll those behemoths across the table." Her relief at his offer was palatable.

Saturday morning, a week later, Sage met Brad at the church. She'd gone back to work for a few days while gifts accumulated. Two days later, he was holed up in his garage making stands. Lucky for him, he'd inherited his father's tools. Sage had let him know the stands wouldn't arrive in time.

It was December first and she'd organized volunteers to start wrapping. With only twenty-three days left, they had to get busy. Donations were rolling in and if they continued at this rate, they'd have just enough gifts to meet everyone's needs. With luck, cash donations would cover gifts for older teens who were often forgotten by donors.

She spent her evenings alone in the church wrapping gifts for those under two years old. Each was labelled with what was inside. Thank heaven for sticky notes.

She pulled into the unusually busy church parking lot and, after a bit of effort, found a space for her small car. It was busier than she expected. There was even a firetruck in the lot, though it appear unoccupied. She grabbed her purse and her paper shopping bag of cookies and hurried up the church's front steps. She opened the door to a riot of noise so loud she halted in her tracks.

"What on earth?" She stepped inside, wiped her boots, and headed toward the basement. The closer she got, the louder the noise. She entered the wrapping room and froze. Chaos reigned.

Christmas music played over the speakers, people darted back and forth laughing. The center space was piled high with unwrapped gifts and all the tables were manned by people busy wrapping. She glanced from person to person. Paramedics and fire fighters dominated the room. Even Renna was here with her leg propped up on a chair. Great to see that her friend's cast was finally gone. They really needed to make time to catch up.

Overseeing everything, Brad, wearing a Santa hat, moved from table to table chatting and dropping off supplies. The scene resembled nothing more than Santa's Workshop. The air even smelled like cocoa and candy canes. Her heart squeezed happily and warmth rushed over her. For a man who was a reluctant volunteer, he sure was getting into the spirit of things. She took a moment to enjoy his perfection. Neatly combed and trimmed dark brown hair. Snug jeans that cradled his backside. Denim shirt that stretched over his shoulders. Most appealing was his smile as he visited each table. He was loving this. Maybe he was finding his Christmas spirit.

Someone had the foresight to bring in a portable coat rack and she hung her jacket up alongside at least twenty others. She turned to join in the merriment.

Brad was right behind her. "Oh! You startled me."

"Good morning," he greeted her.

"Morning. You're up early. Did you organize this? I have volunteers coming, but not for another half hour." She smiled at him as she fumbled for words to thank him.

"I figured the more hands the better. Or is that the merrier." He shrugged. "Of course, if there's a fire, half of these volunteers will be abandoning us. We're on call. Never off duty."

"Oh, that's okay. I'm just happy for the help. I was going to set up a coffee station." She headed for the kitchen.

"Already done. I found an enormous percolator and set it to brew. It should be finished about now. Any snacks in that bag?" He feigned peering into shopping bag.

"There might be cookies. If you're good," she teased.

"I assure you, I'm very good."

She gasped at the double entendre and got a sudden whiff of his cologne. Spicy and deep. Delicious.

"Um. I didn't mean to..." he stammered. "I apologize." He stuffed his hands in his pockets and jiggled his keys.

She put her hand on his arm. Warmth seeped through his shirt, heating her chilled hand. "Relax,

Brad. I know you didn't mean it the way it sounded."
Okay, maybe I wanted you to mean it, but I won't hold you to it, because I'm not looking for a man in a dangerous job.

"I appreciate that. Though, for the record, I like you. Maybe we can get dinner sometime?" Someone called his name and he hurried off before she could decide or answer.

Chapter Six

Brad's hand was warm against her back as he and Sage followed the hostess to a table in the rear of Archie's, one of Cherry Lake's top dining spots. They'd closed up the church after the day's wrapping and were sharing a celebratory dinner together. The large group of volunteers had made short work of the first batch of gifts.

Sage tried not to stare or look like a gawking hick as they made their way past other tables. She wasn't a stranger to a nice restaurant, but she wasn't expecting Archie's to be so fancy. The lighting was low, quiet chatter rippled through the room.

Discrete sound baffles hung from the ceiling to dull the noise and keep conversations private. Candles in hurricane lamps lit each table. The tablecloths and napkins a pale celery green. Simple pastoral scenes decorated the brick walls creating an upscale relaxed but intimate atmosphere. She almost balked at the romanticism of it all.

"You folks are lucky. Tonight marks the launch of Archie's Christmas menu. This week's featured countries are Thailand, the Ukraine, Mexico, and Canada."

"Sounds interesting," Brad said. "What does that entail?"

"You can choose a traditional Christmas meal for any of those countries, or select individual dishes from their menus. Next week, we are featuring four different countries."

"That's fabulous. I can't wait to see what the dishes are," Sage declared.

"There are also a steak and chicken specials for the less adventurous. Your server will be right with you. Enjoy your meal." She handed them single sheet paper menus.

"This is lovely." Sage continued her subtle study of the restaurant.

"I haven't been here before. It's more intimate than I expected. I apologize for that," Brad said.

Her brain reeled. Did that mean he didn't consider this a date? Or that he did but maybe too much intimacy too soon? She thought it was a casual dinner between two coworkers, but part of her heart whispered date, and a soft warm glow wrapped her body and heart.

"Don't fret. I've heard good things, great things, about the food here. I've been wanting to come for ages. Funny that nobody mentioned it was so romantic."

"We don't have to stay if you're uncomfortable."

"Can I ask a question?" She didn't wait for his answer. "Is this just two coworkers getting together, are we friends, or is this a date?" She hoped the dim lighting hid the heat flushing her face.

"Honestly? I'm not sure I know. We are coworkers, co-volunteers. I'd like to think we're becoming friends. But in truth, part of me hopes this is a date. I like you, Sage. You're a beautiful intriguing woman who I'd like to get to know better." He paused. "But, if that makes you uncomfortable, this can be whatever works for you. I don't want to come on too strong or seem like a creep." His smile was soft and reassuring.

"I appreciate the honesty. Can we just let this be whatever it is without a label?" She winced internally at the wimpy question. Especially since part of her wanted to slid closer and wrap her arms around him and test the softness of his hair. Maybe kiss him.

He tilted his head left and winked with his right eye. "Sure thing, kiddo. I'm good with that."

"Kiddo? You do realize that I'm thirty-seven, right?"

"Really? I never would have guessed that. You've got such a young air about you. Youthful confidence. Of course, since you're a year older than I am, I might have to start calling you Granny."

She couldn't stop her laugh. "Maybe I'll call you Kiddo, or Baby-faced Brad." A comfortable sense of camaraderie mixed with a spine-tingling anticipation filled her. Like that fraction of a second when she was perched at the top of a rollercoaster waiting for the exhilarating fall and double-loop. Terrifying in a safe way.

"Do not call me Baby-faced Brad in front of the guys," he warned with a mock scowl.

"Sure thing, B.F.B."

Their server arrived to take their drink orders. Brad ordered a bottle of wine.

"Oh, that's my favorite white," she said.

"I'll remember that. Have you decided what you'd like for dinner?" Brad asked.

"I haven't even looked at the menu. You've been distracting me." She picked up the sheet and started rereading the selections.

"You find me distracting? Good to know," he teased.

Her pulse raced. There was something special about a man who could give and take with jokes and silly comments. Knowing he was interested in her was, to use an old word, titillating.

"I think I'll have the combination from Thailand," Brad said. "I've never tried any of the dishes."

"I am absolutely starved, I missed lunch, so I think I'll have the Thai Mango sticky rice hot and sour soup; the Mexican tamale and the Bacalao which is dried, salted codfish. Definitely some Ukrainian perogies and a cabbage roll. Then maybe some turkey with gravy and finally, some gold old pumpkin pie.

"That's one heck of a combination. It's going to give you an upset stomach."

"Nothing gives me an upset stomach. Not even cherry cheesecake and orange Crush." She laughed when he winced at the combination. "What can I say? I was on a road trip with my folks and it sounded good. I'll try anything once."

"I'll remember that," he teased.

After they ordered, she asked the question that had burned in her mind since they hooked up for the toy drive. "What's your favorite Christmas memory? Do you have one?"

"I do. Tell me yours first," he said.

"That's easy. I remember when I was a kid. Maybe ten. My grampa was away. He served in the Canadian Army. He was due to retire but was involved in Kuwait. Just before the holidays, Nanna got a call saying he was missing. The next ten days were the worst of my life. Bar none. Grampa was my hero. I couldn't bear losing him."

He reached out and squeezed her hand. The simple touch was comforting. "I'm sorry to hear that."

"Thanks. We worried for two weeks, and when you're ten and your favorite grandfather is missing, time creeps by so slowly. On Christmas Eve, Gramma got another call. It was him! He'd been rescued the day before. He was wounded, but not seriously. By Boxing Day, he was home with us. Only for a few days, but it was the best four days of my life. What started out as the worst Christmas became the best one. Ever."

She'd never forget the devastating sense of loss when the bad news came in. Nor would she forget the incredible relief when he was found. When he showed up at home with a broken collar bone, a dislocated and reset shoulder, and two black eyes. It had scarred and scared her. "I didn't know much about marriage back then, but I made a vow never to get involved with a man in a dangerous job. Watching my grandmother's stress and feeling her own terror was too much to live through again."

She studied Brad. He was such a great guy. Almost perfect. Except his job. She'd keep their relationship casual. No romance. She ignored the little devil on her shoulder that said a bit of danger wasn't always a bad thing.

Brad didn't comment on her youthful vow, but his brows did pinch together and he released the hand he'd been holding and straightened up.

"Now, tell me your story," she said, hoping that listening to Brad would make it harder to hear the little voice in her ear whispering for her to take a chance on him despite the hazardous nature of his job.

"It's funny. Your best Christmas was also your worst. Mine too." His eyes got a soft look. "I was nine and fascinated by science. All I wanted was the chemistry set that Billy Peters got for his birthday. He did some great things with that set. He mixed reagents and things frothed and foamed, or changed colors. He managed to set some stuff on fire, quite by accident." His voice was wistful. "Man, I wanted that set."

"Did you get it?"

"I woke up extra early Christmas morning. Nobody else was awake. I snuck downstairs to see if Santa had arrived. Of course, he had. There was a shining brand-new bike and a couple of big packages under the tree. I'm an only child; I knew they were all for me. Well, one or two might be for my parents." He chuckled. "But I couldn't wait to dive in."

"I snuck back upstairs because I wasn't supposed to peek. I went to the washroom, and flushed the toilet. Mom slept like a rock; she could sleep through a hurricane. Dad was a light sleeper and the slightest sound would wake him up. I swear he was always more excited about Christmas than I was. I knew the toilet would wake him, and he'd wake Mom, and I wouldn't get into trouble."

"I remember those days. When nothing beat the anticipation of unopened gifts."

"Those were the days."

His fond smile was so handsome she reached out and grasped his hand. "What happened?"

"We opened all the gifts, except one. It was too big to be the chemistry set. Before Christmas, Dad had warned me that Mom wouldn't like the idea of a chemistry set, but I ignored him and hoped anyway. Seeing that last box and knowing it wasn't my dream gift, I was devastated, but pretended I wasn't. They weren't fooled. Dad convinced me to open the last gift. I did, just so I could go back to bed and sulk."

"Bit of a brat, were you?"

"Totally spoiled in all ways. I was a late baby and Mom catered to my every whim. Except the chemistry set." He laughed at himself. "Anyway, the box was about three feet long, eighteen inches wide, and four inches high. The gift inside changed my life." He leaned back and sipped his water.

"You can't stop there. Tell me what it was."

"Maybe on our next date. If you're good."

"To quote your comment the other day, "I'm very good"." She managed not to blush. "Tell me what it was. What could possibly change your life?"

"Okay. I peeled back the paper. Slowly so I didn't rip it."

"You did not!"

"I ripped it open in a childish pout. Under the wrap was a plain, unmarked cardboard box."

"Brad," she warned.

"I flipped it open. Inside was a bow and six arrows. Not a toy. The real deal. An actual compound bow. At the time, I wasn't thrilled. But once Dad took me to the indoor archery range, I loved it. I lived with that thing. I took classes and private lessons. I joined a team and entered competitions. I was good. My first instructor said I was a natural. I'm not sure if it's true of not, but I won a lot of competitions. Once, I even managed the classic Robin Hood move of shooting one arrow right into the center of the other. I was provincial champ in seven age groups over the years. In grade twelve, I took third at nationals." His voice wasn't prideful, it was chill, like he was simply stating facts.

"You must have been so proud."

"I was. I still am. That unwanted gift gave me drive and determination. In the end it was much more valuable than a chemistry set."

She laughed.

"And that's how my worst Christmas ended up being my best. I'm not saying I didn't light things on fire, or burn up a few things, or make toxic chemical combinations, what teenage boy doesn't?"

"Ever get caught or arrested for those things?" She asked.

"Caught, more than once. Thankfully, I was never arrested. How about you?"

"Not arrested, but I was hauled into the police station once when my brother and I got caught egging a neighbor's house. Scariest day of my life. It was

Halloween, and Mom threatened to cancel Christmas." She shuddered. "Sometimes my mom who is the kindest person on earth...well sometimes she has a mean streak. Your mom must have been terrified of you burning something."

A crazy idea hit her. "Is that why you became a firefighter? Because you're secretly a pyromaniac?"

"My final coach was also a fireman. I wanted to be exactly like him. Community minded, helpful, kind. I followed in his footsteps and joined up at nineteen. What led you to being a receptionist."

"Medical assistant, actually. My path was similar to yours. My aunt was my favorite person, after my grandfather. She was a hospital unit clerk. She took me to work on Bring Your Daughter to Work Day. I found it fascinating. Dealing with the other staff and helping out struck a chord with me and my life path was set."

"Do you like it?"

"I love it. I'm useful. I get to work with people. On rare occasions, I get to assist the doctor. I get to cuddle babies and help pregnant moms. It's fabulous. Well, except when the odd person loses their lunch in the waiting room." She mock gagged.

"Do not talk about that before dinner. The result might not be great."

The rest of their dinner conversation was casual and friendly. They both loved movies from the seventies to the nineties. Cozy mysteries were a shared interest. She loved Star Wars; he preferred Star Trek. Neither of them were big fans of romantic comedy movies, though she watch the occasional one with Renna.

Back outside, the sky was clear, the temperature bone chilling.

"Yikes. It's freezing."

"Good thing I remote started my truck. She should be warm by now." He grasped her arm and helped her navigate the sidewalk. Most of it was clear but the odd patch shone like it might be icy.

The climbed in. "Oh, this is so nice." She held her hands in front of the blasting heater.

"It's still early," he said. "Did you want to grab a coffee? I know a great place to sit and watch the night sky."

"If it's okay, I'd rather just go home and sit by the fireplace. Would you like to join me?" Dinner tumbled about in her stomach like butterflies in the wind. She was unaccountably nervous for his answer. She'd already decided they'd never be more than friends...but a tiny romantic part of her was screaming for more.

"That sounds nice."

The short drive home lasted an eternity and flew by in an instant. She was giddy with excitement and stunned silly with trepidation. What was wrong with her? She was a competent, confident woman. She'd dated before.

This wasn't dating.

Right! She'd forgotten that part. This was friendship. Nothing more.

Her nerves danced as they climbed the stairs to her second-floor apartment. What would he think of her home? What if she wanted to kiss him?

Chapter Seven

Sage's apartment was in one of the newer complexes in town. Brad had seriously debated living there but, in the end, had purchased a home in a family-centric subdivision close to the station.

She unlocked both the deadbolt and the door handle. Interesting. Cherry Lake was a safe little town. He'd have expected only one lock, but wholly approved the extra security. Women couldn't be too careful.

"Come on in." She hung her jacket on a wooden coat rack to the left of the door and placed her high heeled boots on the mat beside it.

Soft light glowed from the kitchen giving the entry a warm, welcoming feel, something that his own home lacked. Maybe he should leave a light on sometimes. He glanced around taking in the details. A full shelf of books sat alongside a shelf of DVD's. Television series, and movies from the look of it. To the left of her gas fireplace, she had a cozy green chair, big enough for two to cuddle in. A chair that gave him ideas, as did the plush carpeting.

The two-seater couch was leather, as was the recliner. He could make out three doors down the hallway. Must be bathroom and bedroom, but there were no lights on in that direction, so he stemmed his curiosity.

The drapes were closed, though he knew they covered French doors to the deck. The coffee and end tables were free of clutter except candles and books. Each chair had a blanket draped over the back. One was wool, knitted maybe. One was fuzzy fabric and the final one was a pieced quilt.

"Did you make the quilt?" he asked. "My mom used to quilt. I have several of her quilts." He'd packed them away in acid free tissue as the quilt shop suggested. Maybe he should use them instead.

"I did not. Mom's the quilter. She teaches classes at a quilt shop in Edmonton. I'm hoping to lure her and Dad here for their retirement. Did you want decaf?"

"Either is good. I've developed a tolerance to caffeine. It comes from all the random shifts. Some nights we sleep, some we don't even rest, though those nights are rare."

She padded n her stocking feet to the kitchen. When they had finished up at the church, he'd waiting in the car for her to change from her dusty work clothing into something else. Later, in the restaurant, he hadn't gotten a good look at her legs under her short skirt. But now? Wowsa! She was fit and trim.

Helpless to stop himself, he followed her after shedding his own coat and boots. "I love your place. I like the gray walls." All the walls were the same light gray, except the one which housed the patio door and the small window by the dining table which was a much darker gray.

Like the rest of the apartment, the kitchen was clutter free. No dishes in the sink, not even a cup or spoon. Nothing on the counters except a knife block and a bowl of fruit. The bowl was white with raised painted grapes and lemons on it. A black and white cat clock with moving tail and eyes hung on the wall. The simple decorations kept the room from seeming sterile. It seemed his new friend and coworker wasn't much for extras. Now that he thought about it, the only jewelry she wore was a small plain band on her right ring finger, and a simple cross necklace. She didn't even wear earrings. Even Renna who was basically one of the guys down at the station wore more jewelry than that.

He watched as she make a couple large mugs of coffee with her Keurig. She fixed his just the way he liked it. She must have taken note when they made coffee at the church.

"Come sit down." She gestured to the living room with her mug. If he tried that, he'd have spilled coffee everywhere. She turned on a couple of lamps. "Sit anywhere you like."

She lowered herself to the couch and nestled in the corner with her legs under her, her body slightly turned to the center. He took that as an invitation to join her.

He sipped his coffee carefully, because it was still blisteringly hot, but he was at a loss as to how to strike up a conversation. Now that he was in her home, he wanted to know everything about her. But more than that, he wanted to kiss her. His instant and unflagging attraction to her was unusual for him.

Sage fidgeted with her hair, and shifted on the seat like she couldn't get comfortable.

"I'm a bit nervous," he said. "I don't know what to talk about."

She giggled. "Me too."

Silence fell again. He hadn't felt this awkward since high school. "What brought you to Cherry Lake?" he asked at last.

"Nothing in particular. I'd been here a couple times as a kid. We used to go camping every summer. Last year, I drove through on my way to Grand Prairie. When my current employer retired, the new owner of the clinic restructured everything. I lost my job. One of those employment apps suggested this position. I figured, why not. How about you?"

"I'm a lifer." He chuckled. "My mom and dad came here when I was an infant. I stayed until I went to training. I worked other places, but came back after my folks passed. I sold the family home, bought something new."

"That's tragic. Sorry you lost your family."

"Thanks. I miss them a lot. But being much older parents, they had a lot of health issues. I'm content knowing they are no longer in pain and are in a better place. Still, I couldn't bear to live in the house I grew up in. A wonderful family lives there now. My house is only a couple years old; I bought it new. I'm hoping to raise my own family there."

He snapped his mouth shut. Why had he said that? Hopefully she didn't feel like he was probing or pressuring her into dating. Damn his errant brain.

"So, you're planning a family then? Me too. I'm not in a rush, though my mother thinks I should step up my search for the perfect man." She groaned. "I'd rather just let life take its course and date when I stumble upon the right man. Do you know what I mean?"

"What constitutes the right man?" *And do I qualify?* He kept the last part to himself. To his surprise she didn't hesitate to answer.

"Solid and dependable. Good sense of humor. Good with kids. Wants a family. Employed. Doesn't live in someone's basement."

Internally, he celebrated. So far, he met all the criteria.

"Safe career. No Danger Dans for me. I want a man who'll be home every night. Not a soldier like my grandfather. Not a missionary like my brother's ex-wife."

And boom! He no longer fit the bill.

"I suppose strong and fit and good looking are points of consideration, but not deal breakers."

"I can bench press two-fifty."

She swatted his arm, exactly the way his mother used to when his dad teased too much.

"Goof ball. You're in a dangerous job. That takes you out of the running. You are firmly in the friend zone, and I'm glad to have you there."

"Happy to oblige," he lied. "Want to watch something on TV. It's still early and tomorrow's Sunday. I don't need to be at church until eleven."

"I'll be right back." She walked down the hall and through a doorway. Two minutes later she came back in a pair of those yoga pants and an oversized sweatshirt. Her pretty dress vanished. Strange, she was equally attractive in casual clothing as she was dressed for dinner.

They settled on a movie. "I like to watch in the dark. Makes it feel like a comfortable theatre." She flipped off all the lights except the one in the kitchen.

He stretched his arm out on the back of the couch, hoping for a feel of her hair. Creep move, one hundred percent, but if he was demoted to the friend zone, he'd take every liberty he could get away with, and not fret over it. Not too much anyway. He pulled his arm back to his side.

"It was okay up there," she glanced up at him as the opening credits to the newest *Christmas Vacation* rolled past. "Make yourself comfortable."

They talked and laughed about the movie's flaws and corny parts. About the midway mark, her head dropped back onto his arm. A sideways glance showed she was asleep. He should go. He reached out and brushed a strand of blonde hair off her cheek. It was silky soft and he had to force himself to let go.

"I should go," he whispered but didn't move. Twenty minutes later she shifted and leaned into him. Another shift and she was nestled against his side, right where he wanted her. "Nope. Not leaving now," he thought happily. He planned to stay right here until she woke up.

Chapter Eight

Sage's head rested on Brad's shoulder and his arm cradled her to his side. Her conscience whirled with silent recriminations. *I'm a horrible person. I can't believe I'm faking sleep just to cuddle up to Brad.*

If he noticed she was faking, she'd be mortified. She'd have to leave town.

What kind of person does this? I'm such an idiot.

Her brain ran riot. She was so caught up in her thoughts that she couldn't hear the movie anymore, the sound had become a low drone against her internal confusion. His arm rested along hers, his fingers stationary just above her elbow. His chest rose and fell in a soft comforting motion. She felt safer here than she had with any man besides the males of her family.

He was comfortable to be around, but a persistent sense of wanting more nagged at her. They'd been working together less than two weeks and part of her felt like she'd known him all her life. She even recognized his scent. Leather, spice, soap, all mixed with something unique and male and pure Brad.

She shouldn't feel so attracted. They barely knew each other, yet it felt like she'd known him all her life. At the same time, it was as if she'd been waiting on him forever. She wiggled again. Snuggling closer.

How did he not realize that she was feigning sleep?

Unless...he wanted her to cuddle in closer.

She didn't dare hope that was the case. That idea led to heartache. Tonight was a one off. Her and Brad together was temporary at best. After this, she'd back away. She would resume her distance and seek out a man who didn't risk his life on a regular basis. Right now, he was too much for her to resist.

Something about Brad drew her in. Like a child to candy. A dieter to cake. She knew she shouldn't but she was going to anyway. Consequences be damned. She sighed at her own folly, and tipped her head down slightly to peek her eyes open and watch the show. After only a minute, she closed them again. Who cared about a movie when heavenly bliss was right under her chest. She could spend the rest of her life right here.

"Hey, Sage." A deep voice penetrated her cozy dream of holding Brad's baby in her arms.

"Mm," she mumbled.

"Sage, honey. Wake up. It's almost eight."

She struggled to open her eyes and orient herself. She was laying on the couch, facing the TV. Someone had draped a quilt over her. A warm male arm was nestled over her and her head was on his ...

She bolted upright. Holy mistletoe! She'd fallen asleep. Her head was on Brad's lap. She jerked to her feet and stared at him. His grin was roguish. He winked and heat flooded her face.

"Morning. Did you have a good sleep?" he asked.

She yawned. "Um. Yes?" She licked her dry lips. "Sorry I fell asleep on you."

"No worries. I enjoyed the movie and having you beside me. You kept slipping lower down, I didn't have the heart to wake you, so I let you sleep. I gave you a pillow to make you comfortable." He patted the throw pillow on his lap.

"You stayed awake all night rather than wake me? That's crazy. You should have given me a shove." Holy

Christmas, she'd slept with her head in his lap. She tried not to let her chagrin show.

"I slept off and on. I'm used to catching catnaps and it's not often I get to doze beside a beautiful woman. I feel remarkably rested." He tossed the cushion aside and rose to his feet. "I only woke you because you mentioned having plans today."

"Thanks. I'll make coffee." She stood and dropped the quilt to her feet and scurried to the kitchen. She was fumbling to open the box of pods when she heard him step up behind her.

His hands landed lightly on her shoulders and she jerked, dropping the box. The pods spilled over the countertop and rolled onto the floor.

"Nervous?" he asked. "Don't be." He gently turner her around. "I enjoyed our dinner last night, and I enjoyed spending the night with you. You're a lovely woman, Sage. One I'd like to get to know better."

"Last night was nice." His wince made her rephrase. "Dinner was amazing. I enjoyed talking with you. It was a lovely evening. We have a lot in common. I didn't mean to abandon you by falling asleep." She stared at the untucked tails of his dress shirt rather than look at him directly.

He eased her chin up until their eyes met. "No shame in being tired and if I wasn't comfortable, I would have gone home." His gaze travelled from her eyes to her lips and back again.

It was all she could do not to kiss him. Heat flared in his eyes and she leaned toward him. He inched closer.

This was it! They were going to kiss. She could hardly wait. No! She needed to stop this. But, maybe just one. She almost rolled her eyes at her dithering. Instead, she inched forward.

Low beeping sounded, distracting her from her self-argument. It grew louder with every beep. It took ten full seconds for it to penetrate the fog of desire clouding her mind. Her alarm!

She blinked twice and backed away. "That's my alarm," she explained needlessly. "I have to get ready. I totally forgot; I'm meeting a friend."

"Male or female?" he growled. His brows pinched together in the middle and turned down on the outside.

"Not that it's any of your business, but a female." His jealousy tickled up her spine like a wave of sweet heat.

"Can I see you after church?"

"Why don't you message me later? I don't know what we're doing or how long it will take." She was going for lunch with Renna, but he didn't need to know that. It never hurt to keep a guy on his toes. It wasn't that she didn't want to see him. Quite the opposite. But she didn't want to seem too eager.

Sometime during the night she'd made the decision to give a relationship with Brad a chance.

"If I don't see you today," she said, "I'll be at the church tomorrow morning making lists of what we have, and what we need. You could stop by."

His frown slowly transformed into a smile that carried all the way to his blue eyes, making them shine. "I'll message you after church. Now, how about that coffee? Do you have time?"

She glanced at the quirky black and white cat clock above the sink. "I have time for a quickie."

He coughed.

"Not that type. Get your mind out of the gutter Putnam. A quick coffee." She turned around to hide her grin. She started the first cup while Brad scooped up the pods that landed on the floor.

Coffee made, she opened the heavy blinds over the dining room window and early morning sunshine flooded in. "I love this view." He joined her at the window. "Don't you just love looking at the playpark, then the football field, and the forest beyond. Her apartment faced nearly due east and the distant trees were the boundary to a provincial park that ran right through town. "Oh, it snowed. There are no tracks in the park. It is pristine." She paused. "That's a little sad. Parks should have tracks running everywhere."

"It is pretty though." He sat at the table as she soaked up the sun. "You love the sun, don't you?"

"I do. I stand here every day and get a bit of sun. In summer I keep the window open except on the hottest days. I get evening shade which helps generate a cool breeze." She shivered. "Of course, when it's this cold, I enjoy my sun and close the drapes back up. No sense chilling the whole place."

Brad watched her stretch her arms over her head and lean left and right. She had curves that would make a dead man sit up and drool. She was fit and sexy. She woke up happy, which was a bonus in his mind. Not that a person could control that, but he worked with a couple guys who were surly until they downed a pot of coffee and breakfast. He much preferred the happy riser.

Last night they'd talked for hours at the restaurant. They had a lot in common. She was quick witted and could converse about anything. What impressed him most was that she was a good listener and could ask just the right question to clarify a detail, or help him understand his own feelings better.

She slid into the chair opposite him and sipped her coffee. "Is there anything that tastes as good as the first morning sip?" she asked.

He'd bet her lips were tastier, but knew better than to put the thought out in the open. He couldn't control his thoughts, but he could control what came out of his mouth. "It is delicious."

They drank quickly and before he knew it, he was standing outside her door. He whistled his way downstairs to his truck. Today was going to be a good day. He had time for a quick shower, and a stop at the station before church.

They shared a delicious Sunday meal of rotisserie chicken, Ceasar salad, and apple pie later that evening.

Without meaning to, he called her every day and asked her out. Sometimes she agreed, others, she declined. Slowly over the next couple weeks, they got to know each other better. With every hour they spent together, he fell further and further. She was fast becoming an integral part of his world. He had no idea what he'd do if she pushed him back into the friend zone after the toy drive was over.

Sugar Cookie Kisses

Chapter Nine

December seventeenth dawned bright and bitterly cold. Sage bundled up and headed for the firehall. Today was the day for taking stock and shopping to fill in any gaps in gifts. She was meeting Brad at the firehall.

It was a good thing she'd walked over because the street out front was full. There were no parking spots left. She nearly tripped over a string of Christmas lights as she made her way into the station.

"Hello," she called out. After a moment she called out again as she walked down the hallway, following the sound of voices.

"Oh. Hi," Brad greeted her. "You're early."

She glanced at her watch. "Actually, I'm ten minutes late. I lost track of time." She'd been reading an Audrey Carnes Christmas rom-com, but she wasn't going to tell him that.

"Well, come in. We're decorating." He waved expansively at the firefighters and medics all busily sorting or placing ornaments. Renna sat in the corner untangling lights. The chief stood beside a half-lit tree, good-naturedly nagged her to hurry up.

"I can see that. I'd ask what the occasion was, but I know you'd just joke about it being Christmas."

"Here hold this." He handed her the end of a light string and climbed a ladder with the other end in his hand. "We're celebrating Christmas." He looked back and winked. "But also, this weekend is the family Christmas dinner for the hall. All the guys and gals are bringing their family for a big turkey dinner. The hospital ladies' auxiliary are cooking for us. There'll be a visit from Santa, and small gifts for the kids. It'll be a blast. You should come."

While the party sounded like fun, and who could resist turkey dinner, she didn't care for the offhand, last-minute invite.

"I know it's short notice. I totally forgot or I'd have asked you weeks ago. Please join us." He stepped down off his ladder and grasped her hands. "Please."

Something in his eyes said he was genuinely sorry for forgetting to invite her. "When is it, and what can I bring?"

"The afternoon of the twenty-second. It starts at two. Dress is business casual meets going to dinner." He grinned. "The ladies like to dress up and bit and they wrangle their men into dress shirts and ties. Not too fancy, there will be games and some might involve being on the floor."

"Might or will?" she teased.

"I have no idea. There was floor time last year; this year I'm not on any of the committees as I've been assigned as your assistant. We'll have to wait and see." He climbed back up. "I'll be ready to go as soon as I string up these lights." She fed him the lights as he moved around the room draping mini-LED lights from small nails already in place. In ten minutes, they were headed for the church.

The basement was aglow with Christmas lights when they arrived. The room smelled of coffee and pine with a faint undertone of cranberry. The minister, his secretary, and Dr. Ingram were already at work.

"Wow, you guys are early," Sage greeted them. "Anyone want a cookie to go with the coffee I smell?"

"You didn't tell me you brought cookies? Which ones? Please tell me you brought sugar cookies. Shortbread are too dry. I'll eat 'em, but sugar are my favorite. Especially with that crystal sugar on top. So delicious." He rubbed his tummy as the others hurried over.

"Bless your soul," the minister said. "The perfect thing to perk me up this morning. Doc and I were up late last night hauling in the last of the bins. We've collected them all. After this final sort, we can shop for what's missing. We'll have to hit it hard to finish in time." His easy grin said he was enjoying every minute of the work.

"Well then, let's get to it." Brad stuffed the last of his cookie in his mouth and strode to the bins of gifts in the center of the room. "Wow, there's a lot here. I'm impressed with Cherry Lake's generosity."

Despite the size of the pile, they had it sorted and ready to wrap within half an hour. "I guess many hands do make light work," Sage chirped. "I've got a list of what we need." She'd been compiling as they sorted. "Who is in for shopping?" Everyone was eager to help and five minutes later, the list divided between them, they hit the stores.

"Mall?" Brad asked.

"You bet. We've some book requests, and The Accessory Shop is giving us a deal on hair stuff for the girls."

"And we can hit the toy store! I love the toy store."

"You're just a big kid, aren't you?" She loved this playful side. Funny how when she met him, he seemed a bit grumpy and now he was as eager an elf as she could want.

"Guilty as charged."

The mall was a zoo despite it being a Wednesday. Usually, she avoided the mall during late December, but today, with Brad at her side the mall seemed full of wonder and excitement.

"Look at the decorations." She pointed at the sparking stars and snowflakes hanging from the ceiling. They stood looking down over Santa's village where a long line snaked through a winter wonderland. The air above them looked like a blizzard amongst the stars.

"Let's get our picture taken with Santa." Brad grinned at her.

"Are you kidding, look at that line. We'd be there for hours."

"Not if you plan ahead. You can book appointments online."

She tapped her finger on her lip. "If only we'd done that."

Brad laughed. "I did. I took a chance that we'd end up here. Come on, Sage. It's our first Christmas together. Let's make a memory. Start a tradition."

He was more excited than most of the children in the line below them. "What the heck. Let's do it. What time is our appointment?"

"We have forty-five minutes to shop. Then Santa. Then we'll get back to shopping. Unless we need lunch."

"You planned it all out, didn't you?"

"Indeed, I did. I've even finishing my Christmas shopping and wrapping. Wait until you see what I got you!"

Holy cranberries. It hadn't occurred to her to get him a gift. Her mind spun through possible ideas until they got to the book store. "They should have baskets. I need dozens of books."

"I'll be your Sherpa. You pick, I'll carry." He held out his arms like he was waiting for her to pile things on.

"Okay. If the load gets too big, we'll figure out what to do."

He followed her around the store. Occasionally, he made suggestions, most of which were very insightful. After twenty minutes, he said, "I'll go find a place near the register for these. I'll be right back."

He wasn't back immediately, and when she finished the last few items on her list, she searched the aisles for him. She found him, in the section for art and coffee table books, chatting with an elderly gentleman. She approached so Brad would see her, but didn't interrupt the conversation. They were eagerly discussing antique fire engines and which represented the greatest jump in technology in one remodel. Brad's passion and fire for the subject brought his entire body to life. His facial expression, his body language, everything spoke of happiness. Her heart swelled with love.

She stopped walking. Love? Did she love him?

A slow smile crept over her face. She did love him. She'd been attracted to him since she saw him hanging lights in the firehall window. Each and every time they got together that attraction grew, despite her attempts to keep her distance. Yeah, she was head over heels, break out the mistletoe in love. The moment needed bells, lights, sirens, something more than just the bliss in her heart.

When she looked up again, Brad was smiling at her, the gentleman was gone. How long had she been thinking about being in love?

Brad strode down the aisle toward her. "That's a lovely smile. What are you thinking about?" he asked.

Heat flooded her face. "You."

Wow!

It was crazy that thinking of him made her smile like that. Brad couldn't believe the peace and joy on her face. It echoed the feeling he got every time he thought about her. Sage was it. The woman he hadn't known he was waiting for.

He realized she was the one shortly after they met. Love at first sight? Maybe not, but he'd fallen not soon after. Her happy demeanor. He upbeat smile. Her eagerness to ensure everyone had a great Christmas.

She'd pitched in and helped when he went out with the guys shoveling snow for seniors and those who were less mobile. There was something about her that was irresistible. And right now, here, in the middle of the mall, it was all he could do to keep himself from kissing her. He closed the distance between them.

His phone chimed.

Dang it!

It was their turn with Santa.

Probably for the best because he wasn't much for public displays of affection, at least not kissing. Hand holding, a brief hug, okay. But he definitely didn't want their first kiss to be public.

"Santa time," he proclaimed. "Let's get them to hold the books until we get back."

They hurried from the store and down the mall to Santa's sleigh.

"Really?" the pink haired teenage elf said with a frown. "Adults?"

"I did book the appointment," Brad said. "We'll be fast, I promise. In and out. A quick snapshot." He held his hands together prayer-like. "It's our first Christmas together. Please."

The elf rolled her eyes. "Ya. Whatevs." She opened the rope and they high-tailed it to Santa.

"Well, what have we here?" The pink cheek old guy proclaimed merrily.

"First Christmas," Brad repeated his explanation. "We want to capture it. Forever."

Santa slid to the middle of his sleigh seat. "One on each side then. Make it quick. Kids are waiting." The words were gruff, but his tone cheerful. "Did the same thing with my wife back in the day. We've been together for forty years. I hope this picture, this memory brings you guys all the holiday magic and love."

Brad hoped so too. And judging by the look on Sage's face, she felt the same.

"Santa, you're the best." They hopped up and each slung one arm behind Santa and held hands in front of him.

"Say mistletoe," the photographer called then snapped off half a dozen quick pictures. "One more, with you guys together on one side." They repositioned and he took a few more shots. "See the elf over there," he pointed to an igloo on his left. "He'll give you a jump-drive of your pictures."

The whole thing took less than three minutes. It took longer to preview and pay for the photos than to get them taken. They each tucked their memory sticks safely away and returned to the bookstore.

Brad smiled all the way there. Sage had agreed to the pics without issue and had played along. Now, they had memories for whatever the future brought them. Next year, he'd book their visit early, while the kids were still in school. Despite his joy in having the adorable pictures, he felt guilty for taking up time that was meant for kids.

Sugar Cookie Kisses

Chapter Ten

Brad's Christmas party was a blast. They ate an amazing meal. They played silly games and watched the children open their gifts after they'd all had a chance to sit on Santa's knee.

"We could have gotten our pictures done here," Sage said.

"Where's the fun in that? Besides, I want the whole world to know we're dating. The mall works better for that." He grinned unrepentantly.

She smiled back. There was something super sweet about knowing how much he cared for her. They hadn't traded the L-word yet, but it was only a matter of time. There was no doubt in her mind that it was coming soon, at least from her.

Families were trickling away, one by one. "It's awful quiet in here now," Sage said and leaned against Brad's shoulder. They sat side by side in the games room on the second floor of the hall. There was a ping pong table, a pool table, a couple of video game consoles, and most exciting, a fireman's pole to the truck bay. All the kids had slid down the pole with two fire fighters at the bottom to catch those whose grip might slip. None did, but Sage was relieved by the safety measure. She even took a ride down the pole herself. Thankfully, she had thick tights under her dress, because how was she supposed to resist the opportunity?

"This is more typical of the hall," Brad said. "Just the guys, maybe a guest or two. Killing time until the next call."

"It's actually peaceful."

"Want to play a game? Watch a movie? I can kick your butt in Mario Party."

"Ha. Nobody beats me at Mario. Game on, dude." They moved from the sofa to two chairs which faced the enormous television and gaming systems. "I'm player one," she teased as he fired up the game.

"Now way. I signed us in, that makes me player one." They started a fresh game and began at the beginning.

"Ha. Beat you on that one," Brad gloated with a teasing grin.

Six levels into the game, a call came into the station and the entire hall exploded into action. Fire fighters, medics, supervisors, everyone rushed out. Before she knew what was going on, Sage was alone with the single man left to man the station.

This was it. Her greatest fear, live and in person. Crap on cardboard. The man she'd fallen for was off risking his life and they'd never even kissed. Suddenly all the delicious food she'd eaten earlier jumped into her throat. She raced for the washroom before it was too late.

An eternity later, certain that there was nothing else to lose, she returned to the gaming room and sat twisting her hands together. Her heart raced, her palms sweat, her body was racked with shivers. Tears streaked down her face.

Her grandfather had come back, but what if Brad didn't? Her life would be ruined. By all that was holy, she didn't need this. This pain, this agony, this unbearable waiting was why she hadn't wanted to date Brad. His job would kill her.

"Are you okay?" Pete, the young man left manning the station asked.

"What do I do now?" She buried her face in her hands. "How do I deal with this?"

"I don't know, ma'am," Pete said. He couldn't be more than twenty-one. At thirty-seven, he seemed like a baby to her. "You can wait it out, though depending on the severity, it could be hours. Or, you could go home and I'll have Brad call you when he gets back."

She sighed and brushed away her tears. She couldn't stay here. She had to be somewhere she could distract herself. All the lights and decorations mocked her. Their beauty lost its shine. She needed peace.

"I'll go," she declared and jumped to her feet.

"I'll tell him to call you," Pete called as she hurried past him to find her jacket.

Tempted though she was to search out the fire, she resisted the urge. Seeing a blaze would only make things worse. Bundled up against the cold and snow, she hurried home and climbed onto her treadmill. Music blasting through her headphones, she ran and ran. But no matter how fast she went, or how long she pounded step after step, she couldn't outdistance her fears.

She had to break up with him. She couldn't live like this. Not again. Not after what happened to her grandfather. It didn't matter that Pops came home; it was the uncertainty she couldn't deal with.

Exhausted after a four-hour fight to save a house and protect its neighbors, Brad showered and climbed into bed at the station. He had hoped Sage would still be there, but wasn't surprised to find she'd left.

Though it was late, pushing midnight, he texted anyway.

She didn't answer.

He was still on shift, and couldn't go see her, though all he wanted was to hold her in his arms. Somehow during the fire, he was able to block everything out and maintain his focus, but the minute he stepped into the hall, his brain went into overdrive. He needed to see Sage, to touch her, to reassure himself that she was safe.

They'd saved all five members of the family, as well as their cat and dog. The house was gone, burnt to cinders. Likely due to a dirty or plugged wood burning stove. Didn't people know they had to inspect them yearly? In Cherry Lake, the fire inspector did it for free.

He texted again. Maybe she'd answer. Maybe they could talk. Nothing.

He called. Nothing. After three calls, he gave up and rolled over. Anxiety clawed at his chest. Eventually, pure exhaustion pulled him into sleep, his last thought was that he'd see her tomorrow at the church to finish building the baskets for distribution.

Eyes burning with fatigue, he crawled out of bed, guzzled three cups of coffee, and devoured two muffins brought in by one of the guys coming on shift. He still didn't feel human, but he wanted to see Sage and he'd promised to help out.

Leaning against the kitchen counter, he sent her a direct message to see if she wanted a ride. The icon showed she read it, but she didn't respond. He waited five minutes and messaged again. The icon changed to read.

"Hockey socks!" he blurted without meaning to.

"Wow. Harsh language," his coworker Gibson teased. "What's up?"

"Sage is reading my texts but won't answer them. She ignored me last night too." He paced back and forth and tried not to swear.

"Maybe she's busy. She's got a lot going on with the toy drive. Give her a minute." He started running water in the sink to clean up the breakfast mess. They had a dishwasher, but several of the guys, Brad included, liked to wash and dry by hand.

"I don't know. We sort of fell into dating. She refused to date because she didn't want to be with a guy with a dangerous job. What if last night scared her?" He rubbed the ache in his chest.

"What if it did?" Gibson asked. "What will you do? I can tell you this, not all women are cut out to be fire fighter's wives. It's a tough choice. You're off now. Go find her. Talk to her. But you probably need to be prepared for rejection. I've lost more women to this job…" he trailed off sadly.

♥♥♥

The church basement was bustling when Brad arrived. There had to be thirty people there, all scurrying back and forth. It was chaos. He hung up his jacket and took a moment to take stock of what was happening. Instrumental Christmas music played softly in the background. The minister and his wife waltzed together in the corner, just for a second as they passed one another. The simple gesture of caring touched his aching heart.

Sage was nowhere in sight. He headed toward Renna. "Hey Ren. Have you seen Sage?"

"Brad. How are you? I'm surprised to see you after last night. You guys were out late. How are you holding up?" She scanned a gift tag and hoisted the gift into her arm with three others.

"I'd be better if I could find Sage." He scanned the crowd again.

"I think I saw her head into the ladies' room. I'm sure she'll be back in a second. Here, take these to table eight." She thrust the packages in his arms.

He dropped the gifts off and searched again for Sage. It was time to talk. She was out of sight. She was hiding, he was certain of it. Checking to be certain nobody was looking, he slipped into the ladies' room.

"Sage? Are you in here?" he asked quietly.

"Go away, Brad. This is the ladies' washroom. No men allowed." Her voice came from the furthest stall.

"Are you avoiding me?" He rapped on the stall door.

"I'm going to the washroom. We can talk another time."

He peeked under the door, just enough to see her feet. There was no way she was going to the washroom. She must be leaning against the side wall.

"I can see your feet. You're hiding. Come out. Tell me why you're avoiding me." He heard a sniff and a sigh. The lock snapped open and the door swung inward. She stepped out.

"Oh no! What's wrong?" he asked. Tears streamed down her face. Her eyes were red rimmed. She'd been crying. Probably for a long time.

"Nothing. Everything."

He wanted to pull her into his arms. "Talk to me, Sage. I can't help if I don't know what's wrong." He knew what was wrong. He'd known it since last night.

She shook her head and went to the sink to splash water on her face. "It would be better if you just went home," she mumbled through her hands.

"Is this about my job? Can we talk about it?" he pleaded, not caring that he sounded desperate. "I love you, Sage." *Great time to mention it. Idiot.*

"I-I love you too," she stammered brokenly. "That's the trouble. I can't live knowing you're in danger. I was sick with worry last night. Literally sick."

"The fear gets better. It never goes away, I know that. But I also know that it gets easier to deal with. Talk to the other wives. Please."

"I'm not your wife, Brad. I never will be. I can't deal with the stress. We're done." She dried her hands, straightened her spine, and headed for the door.

He grasped her shoulder and gently spun her around. "Just like that? One little hiccup and you walk? We deserve better. I'm begging you. Don't give up so easily. Cherry Lake has so few fires that it's almost a joke to have a fire department. We do a lot of good work, but fires are rare."

"Seventeen last year. I googled it." She glared at him, her eyes mad and sad all at once. "I can't spend seventeen nights every year in fear. I lived this with my grandfather being missed. I did it last night. I can't, Brad. I just can't." She spun and left the bathroom.

Disappointed and angry, he hauled back his arm to take a swing at something. Anything. Breaking his fist on the wall wouldn't solve anything. Desolate, he stuffed his hands in his pocket and went home. He couldn't be near her without begging. But this wasn't over. Not by a long shot. He'd figure out how to convince her that they were worth a little fear.

Sugar Cookie Kisses

Chapter Eleven

Sage knew she should be elated. The gifts were sorted, wrapped, and boxed for distribution. They finished with one day to spare. Everything would be delivered on the twenty-fourth. Volunteers were organized and scheduled.

She was miserable. After over a month of seeing Brad virtually every day and many evenings, not seeing him sucked. Big time. She cried until she had no more tears, then she cried some more. Why did she have to fall in love with him?

Now, standing in the nearly empty church basement, she wished he was at her side.

"Come on, girl. Time to celebrate," Renna declared after turning out the kitchen light. "Let's go grab some wine and cake."

"Maybe another night. I just want to be alone. I'm exhausted." She struggled into her jacket and tugged her hat down over her ears.

"Oh, stuffing and gravy! Don't be ridiculous. You don't want to be alone. This is the time for companionship." Renna stood, hands on her hips, her red hair bounced in time to the impatient tapping of her foot. "Let's get that cake and wine. We'll go to your place and bash men."

"I don't want to bash Brad. He's a great guy." She sniffed. This hurt so much. Only twenty-four hours and it felt like days, weeks apart.

Renna put her coat on. "Okay, no bashing. But we'll do girl time. Trust me on this. When you lose the one you love, you cry with your friends, not alone."

Reluctantly, Sage agreed and in no time, they were sitting on her couch facing each other, feet in the middle, wine in hand.

"A toast," Renna said. "To a job well done and to finishing it with a bang tomorrow." She raised her glasses.

Sage tapped her glass to Renna's. "To a great team. I just hope we haven't missed anyone."

"Girl, you triple checked with every agency. Every school and church. We got everyone. You know it as well as I do." She sipped her wine.

"I'm going to miss him," Sage blurted, unable to keep her thoughts from Brad for more than a few seconds.

"Wow. That took," Renna glanced at her watch, "eight minutes. You are so done. You need to figure out how to deal with his job or you'll be a spinster for the rest of your life. Did you want me to order you the crazy cat lady starter kit?" she teased gently.

"Funny. Not. What would you do?" She set her wine down and picked up her pumpkin pie. She buried it in a mountain of spray whipped cream.

"I've been there. Loved and lost. It's tough. Ryan and I married right out of high school. We both became fire fighters and worked together. I lost him to cancer five years ago. I still miss him. Every. Damned. Day. I know what you're going through. I would give anything to have Ryan back. Anything."

Sage embraced Renna for a long comforting moment. "I am so sorry for your loss. I had no idea," Sage said at last. What could you say to that? Literally nothing. Part of her felt like a fool for giving up on love after hearing that story. The rest of her was too scared to risk losing him to death. It was better to walk away first.

"What are you going to do? I saw Brad today, before he followed you into the washroom, he's already a wreck."

"I have to do what's right for me. You know that, right?"

"I know that," Renna said sympathetically. "I'm just not sure that you've chose the right thing. I'll stand by you, and support you, no matter what you choose. But reconsider. Give it a few days. Think it over." Renna took a deep breath. "Something to consider is that you love him, and even if you aren't together, he'll be risking his life. The danger doesn't change if you walk away. He'll still be at risk, but if ending it still feels right, so be it. I can't end my relationship, work or personal with Brad. But I'll still have your back."

Sage nodded sadly. She really couldn't ask for more than that. "I'll think it over." Probably a million times, but she knew she wasn't going to change her mind. Ever. Maybe, in time, she'll forget she loves him.

"I'll take some extra shifts over Christmas," Brad told Gibson who was deputy chief of their hall as well as his closest friend. "I can work a double. Maybe a triple if it's quiet."

Gibson leaned back, put his legs on the desk, and gave Brad his what are you up to stare. "You've got enough shifts. Every man and woman who works here signed up for this gig and the crazy hours. Go. Spend time with Sage. I didn't think I'd see you in here unless there was a call."

"She dumped me." He tried, and failed to keep the hurt from his voice. He flopped into the chair across from Gibson. "I thought it was going so well. I even bought this." He flipped a black velvet box onto the desk.

Gibson picked it up and thumbed it open. He whistled. "Nice. Is that an emerald?"

"It is. I wanted something different because she's unique. What do I do with it now? I can't take it back. Who wants to be the idiot that returns an engagement ring."

"So that's it? You're just giving up. One fight. I've never met a married couple who don't have an occasional spat. Hell, my folks fight all the time, but they're still happily married. Relationships take work."

"This, coming from a bachelor," Brad snarled.

"Hey, it's not from lack of trying. Given my druthers, I'd be in a serious committed relationship with a woman eager to pop out some babies. Preferably half a dozen. I want a big family."

Brad shook his head. "I didn't think I wanted a relationship. At least not until I saw Sage standing on the sidewalk staring at me hanging lights. Something struck me about her right away."

"Love at first sight? Impressive. Dude, what are you doing here? Go. Chase her down. Don't take no for an answer."

"I don't know..." Every fiber of his body and soul wanted to run after Sage. But she didn't want him. Being away from him was her choice. He wanted her to be happy. Wasn't that what everyone wanted of the people they loved? Happiness? If she was happy without him, who was he to complain? A little bit of his heart piped up and screamed at him to chase her. His heart beat out a steady rhythm of go-get-her. Go-get-her.

He snatched the ring off the desk. "You know what? I'm not giving up that easily. If she wants this done, I'll abide by that decision. Eventually. For now, I'm giving it all I've got."

"Grand gestures. Women love 'em," Gibson called as Brad hurried from the office.

If she wanted a grand gesture, he'd give her one. And he knew just what to do.

Sugar Cookie Kisses

Chapter Twelve

"I don't know why you needed me for this," Sage grumbled. She walked beside Brad who pushed a dolly holding a stack of late presents the hospital gift shop had collected. Apparently, a few generous people had left gifts even though the box had been collected days ago.

"This is your gig, not mine. If I had to come, you had to come. I still don't know why they called me and not you."

She looked at him out of the corner of her eye. He was as handsome as ever, and more than once on the trip over, she'd caught him watching her with a sad smile on his face. Maybe he missed her as much as she missed him. *No!* She didn't want him sad. She wanted him to get on with his life.

"Sage, have you got a minute?" Ernie Chau, pediatric nurse called out quietly as they walked past the cafeteria on their way out.

She glanced at Brad who nodded agreement. They joined Ernie at his table. "Ernie, what's up?"

"I'm glad you're here. I've got a patient I'd like you to meet."

"Okay. Why?"

Ernie leaned toward them. "She's twelve, she's terrified, her father split when she was diagnosed with leukemia and there's no indication that he'll come back. Her mother has three other children and hardly ever gets to the hospital." He shook his head and his long black bangs flopped forward.

"That's tragic," Sage said. She wanted to cry for the child.

"What can we do?" Brad asked.

"I know electronics aren't usually part of the Christmas drive, but if you could get her a tablet, a laptop, an ereader, anything. She's insatiably curious and bored out of her mind. She's new in town and doesn't have many friends."

Brad cursed under his breath, practically taking the words right out of Sage's mouth.

"Are they on the lists?" Sage asked.

"I have no idea, but I doubt it. Fallon, her mom, is very proud and doing her best. She's working nights at Rick's Bar to make ends meet. I think, if you talk to Arista, you'd be able to get the details you need. Subtly of course."

"Of course. I'll be subtle."

"I suggest we approach her about her siblings. They're younger, she'll want them to have a good Christmas," Ernie said.

"Consider it done," Brad said. "That girl will get her laptop if I have to buy it myself." He slapped a hand on the cafeteria table and everyone turned to look.

Ernie waved away their attention and most eyes returned to their meals or companions. Five minutes later, they stood outside Arista's room.

"Let me just check she's up for a visit," Ernie said. Half a minute later he waved them inside. "Arista, this is Sage and her friend."

"Brad," Sage said when she realized he didn't know Brad.

"They're with the Christmas toy drive," Ernie added.

"Hi," Arista said shyly. She wore a flowered scarf on her head and was thin and pale, but her face was wreathed in an enormous smile. "Ernie says you can get my siblings Christmas presents." The words fell somewhere between challenge and entreaty.

"We'll sure do our best," Sage said. "Tell us about them." How could a child deal with her mortality on a daily basis when Sage couldn't deal with Brad in danger as an adult?

"Davia and Mavis are twins. They're three and both girls. They like Lego, dolls, and toy dishes. Maybe one of those real oven things for them. Billy's five. He likes building stuff and doing experiments." She paused, a tear in her eye. "They gave up so much for me. So did Mom. Can you get something for her?"

"What do you think she needs, or wants." Brad surprised Sage by beating her to the question.

"I don't know. A spa day? The brakes on her car fixed so she doesn't need to ride the bus? Maybe a new winter coat. She gave me hers and won't take it back even though I'm stuck in here." She sighed and closed her eyes. "Anything. Food? Clothing?"

Tears welled in the back of Sage's throat. She swallowed them down before they leaked out of her eyes or she started sobbing. "We'll do what we can. I know some people who might be able to help."

"And she'll never know you asked us to help out," Brad promised, his voice husky. "What would you like?"

"Nothing. Just look after everyone else, okay?"

Ernie spoke up. "You have a rest, Arista. I'll show Sage and Brad out."

"Thanks for talking to us, Arista. We'll do our best," Sage promised. "Rest up and feel better."

Ernie walked them down the hall. Once they were out of earshot he said, "She sold her laptop before she was admitted and bought groceries with the money. Healthcare may be free in Canada, but a single mom with four kids?" He trailed off.

Brad paced back and forth muttering under his breath. "The whole thing is so unfair," he grumbled. "We have to do something."

Sage placed a hand on his arm. "We will. I don't know what yet, but I'll make sure that family has a fabulous Christmas. All of them."

Ernie's personal pager let him know he was needed elsewhere. "Thanks, Sage, Brad. I'll rest easier knowing good things are coming." They watched him stride down the hall. Silently, they returned to the SUV.

"Can we make a quick stop on the way back to the hall?" Brad asked.

"Sure. I've got nowhere else to be today. I'm still off work until after Boxing Day."

He drove carefully down the street and pulled up outside a strip mall. "Wait here. I'll only be a second." He hurried into a costume shop.

Halloween was well over, what did he need a costume for?

He was back in under ten minutes, a red and white suit in a clear bag.

"Santa? Are you going to play Santa?"

"Yes. I'm buying that girl a laptop and Santa will drop it off."

"You've told me a dozen times that you refuse to be Santa. What changed?" She clutched his arm. "Wait. You can't. Not unless you take gifts for everyone." She hated to burst his bubble, but he hadn't thought this through. "However, we might be able to make it appear in the middle of the night."

"But I rented this suit. The most realistic one they had. I have to do something." His frown touched her heart. "I've been to multi-vehicle pileups, major fires, floods, and disasters. Not once in my entire career have I felt this helpless."

"I know. I feel the same." Her chest ached and her eyes burned from unshed tears. "We'll find a way. I promise you."

"I'm stopping for that laptop now. We're ready when we have a plan. I'll set it up with all the programs she might need. Maybe some games? Oh, and one of those educational video apps. The subscription one."

"That would be amazing. If she's as smart and curious as Ernie says, she'll love that. I can't spend that kind of money from the toy drive on one child, but personally I can. Let me help pay for it."

"I'll be the money on this. You find a way to execute it."

She crossed her arms over her chest and gave him her best stare. "Either I help pay, or I don't help execute. Your choice."

"Fine by me. Let's figure out a plan." Something about his expression was smug. She didn't care, she just wanted Arista to have a great Christmas.

"You could be Santa for the hospital drop off. I'm sure Chief Ramirez will happily give up the job. Then we could give her the laptop afterward," she suggested.

He grinned foolishly. "That's perfect. Let's go find out if her family is on the list."

Chapter Thirteen

Sage wasn't ready for this. Today was the last day of the toy drive, and the last time she'd see Brad. Christmas Day. Volunteers had delivered presents all over town. They were worked side by side with other charities who provided food or clothing. Christmas Eve delivery had been a massive effort involving hundreds of people. Dr. Ingram, the minister and his wife, and Chief Ramirez handled the dispersal of everything, except for the gifts destined for the hospital.

Sage and Brad were handling that.

She stood on the sidewalk outside her apartment building enjoying the warmer weather. It was barely below freezing. The air was crisp and clean and blessedly still. Fluffy flakes drifted to the ground. There was something special about snow on Christmas morning that gave her hope for the future.

She heard the rumble of Brad's truck before she saw it come around the corner. Why did men love trucks so much. Of course, today he carried a pickup box of gifts to distribute at the hospital. He pulled to a stop and she hopped into the cab.

"Morning," she greeted him. "Merry Christmas, Brad."

"Good morning and Merry Christmas to you, Sage. You look lovely. Is that a new jacket?" She wore a bright red wool coat. Her hat, scarf, and mitts were patterned like a sock monkey.

"It is new. It's my gift to myself this year."

"No gifts from your family? Either of your brothers, your mother?"

"Oh, yes, there will be. We're getting together on Boxing Day for a couple days. We'll do Christmas then. I'm excited to see them. I just hope the roads are good enough to drive to Drayton."

"I can take you, if you need a sturdier vehicle. My truck's a four by four."

His offer shocked her. She blinked several times until she felt like an owl. "That's very generous of you. I'll consider it." She wouldn't accept but he didn't need to know that.

They made their way through the snow to the hospital. It seemed like seconds until they had everything unloaded and taken to a vacant room in the children's ward. Ernie Chau was meeting them there with a small team of hospital workers dressed as elves. Everyone wanted Christmas to be extra special for the kids.

The floor was buzzing with visitors who came to spend the day with their children. Families with more than one child were asked to bring a gift of two for the siblings to open while the patients did theirs. No sense adding tears to the day.

Brad slipped into his Santa costume in the corner of the room while Sage turned her back. "Can you fix my beard?"

"Sure." She turned around. Her heart stumbled. He looked amazing. Big fat belly. Red velvet jacket and pants. Knee high black boots, real boots, with buckles. Matching belt. He had his wig on, but his face was bare.

"I've got this glue stuff for it, but I can't see to get it in the right place."

"I'll do it." She took the beard and glue. After reading the bottle, she dabbed glue on the beard and lifted it to his face. She couldn't resist touching him just once more. His skin was smoothly shaven, and up close and personal, he smelled of candy canes and cookies. Just like she'd expect Santa to smell. He'd gone all out for the kids. Doubly so since he swore up and down that nobody was getting him into the suit.

She pressed the beard into place and slipped the retaining straps over his ears, just in case. She placed his hat on his head and handed him his gold rimmed glasses. She was grinning like an idiot and didn't care. He looked amazing.

"Are you laughing at me?" he asked, his own grin turning up the corners of his beard, near his mouth. He winked.

A little shiver of happiness went through her. "Not at all. I was just thinking how great you look." She grasped his hands in hers. "Thank you for this. I know we're not on the best terms, but I appreciate you going the extra mile for me."

"We're still friends, Sage. I did this for you."

Ernie snuck into the room. "Ready to go, Santa?"

"Sure thing."

"Give me a second," Sage said. She turned her back to the men and slipped out of her jacket, and not a second too soon, she was melting. She slipped on her own wig and glasses, smoothed her white apron, and turned around. "Mrs. Claus reporting for duty."

Brad and Ernie gaped at her. "You look great," Brad exclaimed, "but much too young to be Mrs. Claus." She grinned back at them.

"We've gathered everyone in the play area. It's cramped, but we'll manage. Mellie went home this morning, so we'll set her gifts aside until she's back tomorrow."

"Let's do this thing." Brad slung a heavy sack filled with individual stockings carefully sealed and labelled onto his back and opened the door. "Ho ho ho. Merry Christmas."

He strode down the hall cheerily greeting everyone. In the playroom, jubilant kids mobbed him. Several little girls swarmed Sage when they couldn't get close to Santa. With a bit of jockeying a lot of ho-ho-hoing, Santa got everyone settled and took his place in a recliner set out for him.

"All right boys and girls. I've got a little something for each of you here, and maybe if you're good, you'll find a gift in your room when we're all finished here. Hang around until the end for cookies and cocoa. Mrs. Claus makes the best sugar cookies ever."

Sage had brough nearly two hundred cookies to the hospital yesterday. Some for the staff, most for the patients who were allowed them. She even made gluten free versions for a couple of sensitive kids. She smiled at Brad, he was playing this to the hilt and doing an amazing job.

He pulled the first stocking from his sack. "Tessa Cooper, come see me."

She climbed onto his lap, her parents snapped a picture and she whispered in his ear. They chatted for a minute, she hopped down and he called up the next child. One by one, they climbed on him, pulling his beard, crushing his arms, once accidentally kneeing him between the legs. Through it all he smiled and kept up the façade, though Sage was sure he'd have bruises the next day.

Each child, and their siblings received a stocking. From the bottom of his sack, he pulled a smaller sack. "Arista, where are you?" he asked.

She walked forward unsteadily, her mother holding her elbow. "This one's for you, sweetheart," Brad said. He patted his knee. "Take a seat and tell me what you want for Christmas."

"I'm too old," she said with a blush.

"Nonsense. Come sit." He whispered something to her and she perched on the edge of her knee. "Where are your sibling?"

She waved them forward and he handed them all stockings, even her mother. Come. Let's get a picture. Ernie stepped forward and snapped a family shot. The staff elves rolled in with trays of nutritious snacks, cocoa, and Sage's cookies.

Sage's heart had never been fuller. When the party broke up, Brad changed back into street clothing. Sage slipped her costume off and used a bulky sweater to cover the light T-shirt she wore over her red and white leggings.

"Let's go visit Arista," she said. "We can give her the laptop while the other kids are busy."

"Knock, knock," Brad said at Arista's door. "Can we come in?"

"Yes!" Arista waved them forward. "Mom, this is Brad, and Sage. They did this." She waved her hand at the gifts her siblings were opening.

Her mother strode toward them. "I'm Fallon. Thank you so much, for all of this." Tears flowed down her cheeks. "I had nothing. Literally nothing for them. You've made this Christmas wonderful. Thanks for making magic."

"Don't thank us, thank Ernie. He called us in," Sage said as she dashed away a few tears of her own. "There's one more gift."

"Two actually," Brad said.

"But there's already so many."

Sage looked at Brad. The only gift she knew about was the laptop. She handed the gaily decorated paper shopping bag to Arista. "This one is for you."

The teen peeked inside and squealed with joy. "A computer!" She giggled, then cried, and laughed some more. "Best Christmas ever."

Once she settled down, Brad handed Fallon a similar bag. "This is for you."

"I can't take that," she waved the gift away, tears falling harder.

"Take it. It's from the guys at the hall and a few of my friends." He shoved the package into her hands. "I won't take no for an answer."

She peeked inside. "Another computer?"

"A little elf told me yours died. There are also some gift cards. One for the garage. One for gas. A couple for groceries and a big box store. They guys at the station have added your rental to their shoveling list. We'll keep your walks snow free this winter."

Fallon flung her arms around Brad. "You two are the real deal. Total Santas. Both of you." She abandoned Brad to hug Sage. "Thank you so much," she whispered brokenly into Sage's ear. "You can't know what this means to me."

Sage oscillated between elation over what they'd accomplished and mourning for this family's plight. Wrapped up in everything were her confused feelings for Brad.

They stuck around for a while to chat with Arista and Fallon while the little ones played with their new toys. Then they took a few minutes to wander around the floor talking to families and double checking that nobody was forgotten.

They bumped into a young boy, about ten with his arm and leg in a cast. "Wow, what happened to you," Sage asked.

"I fell off my snowboard and hit a tree." He winced.

"Bet you don't do that again," his mother said.

"I probably will." He laughed. "You have to try new things. You can't be afraid to do stuff because you might get hurt. I love snowboarding. I did something stupid. I'll still snowboard but I'll be safe. You need to be safe, but take risks. Life's no fun if you're scared and hiding."

His mom shook her head in mock exasperation.

"Dad says it too. Play hard. Play safe, but take risks."

The words, the simple advice wormed its way into Sage's heart. Looking around her it dawned that life was too short to live in fear. She was through being a coward. Love was worth the risk.

As they drove home, Sage mustered up her courage. "Brad, would you like to come in for dinner? I cooked a ham yesterday. There are leftovers."

He glanced at his watch and her heart fell. He was going to make an excuse. She was too late.

He flashed her a smile. "I've got ninety minutes before shift. I'd love to spend it with you. Dinner sounds amazing."

Sugar Cookie Kisses

☐Chapter Fourteen☐

Brad settled down on Sage's small couch. "Are you sure I can't help out there?" he asked. Sage had chased him to the seat with a cup of tea so she could prepare dinner.

"I'm one hundred percent certain. This kitchen is too small for two people."

Her kitchen was perfectly cozy for two people close to each other and he was desperately hoping that her inviting him over was a sign that she was warming up to him and his dangerous career.

She called him to the table a couple minutes later. She'd covered it with a snowman print cloth and set out glasses of water. Three short candles burned in the center of the table. It was incredibly romantic and his heart danced.

Yes! He was back in! He mentally punched the air in celebration. "This looks incredible. Thank you for inviting me."

They ate in virtual silence except for discussing dinner. The urge to ask for an explanation burned in the back of his throat. Instead, he said, "I'm thinking of opening an inspection service. I could inspect houses and businesses and offer safety advice. I've got all the classes I'd need. I did some research. The licensing process shouldn't be too hard."

"Don't you love being a fire fighter?"

"I do. But other things, other people, have made me reconsider my career," he confessed.

"Would you be happy doing that?" She set her fork on the table and stared at him. Her voice was flat and he'd give everything he owned to know what she was thinking.

"I'd be happy. Maybe not as happy as I am now, but the reward would be worth it. I'd do it for you. I love you, Sage, and there's nothing I wouldn't give to make a life with you." He bit back his fear and his fear of being hurt.

His stomach rolled and the delicious food suddenly weighed a hundred pounds. "I know we haven't known each other very long. But I'm in love with you. I can't imagine not being in love with you.

I've adored you since you accepted the eggnog hot chocolate you didn't want just to avoid hurting my feelings. So yes, I'd be happy doing something else, if I had you in my life."

She jumped up from the table and ran down the hallway. She was gone so long he got up to go. His heart was crushed. It would never recover. He blinked back tears. He wanted to storm out of the apartment and bury himself in a bottle. With all the control he could muster, he cleared his empty plate to the sink and walked to the door.

"Wait! Don't leave," she called from the end of the hallway. She strode toward him, a crooked, nervous smile on her face. She thrust a badly wrapped package at him. "This is for you." She grabbed his elbow and pulled him to the couch. "Open it."

She sat beside him, wiggling like an excited puppy. "Open it," she repeated.

"Who wrapped this? An eight-year-old?" he teased.

"I did. Just now. I was in a rush. Technically, it wasn't for you. It was from the toy drive and I'm supposed to return it. It wasn't suitable for a kid." She chuckled. "I'll pay for it because I'm giving it to you.

It's perfect for you. I mean, I do have another gift, a real gift. But this one..." she trailed of. "Just open it, Brad. You'll understand. I promise."

He stared at her, trying to figure out what she was up to. He'd offered to change his life for her and she'd given him a weird package. What did that mean?

This was it. Maybe she was crazy but the boy who said to take chances really touched her. All the bravery amid fear and illness had brought her to her senses. She was through being a coward. Brad was worth the risk. That's why she asked him to dinner. She hadn't intended to give him this gift, but when he said he'd change jobs for her, she'd nearly wept with happiness.

But that wasn't what she wanted. She couldn't crush his joy in his career because she was a coward. She'd adapt. She'd hire help to adapt if that's what it took.

"Will you just open it. Please."

He shook his head. "I don't know. You're making me nervous. You've giving me a stolen present. Is this going to be how a relationship between us goes?" His wink reassured her that he was teasing.

He's as nervous as I am!

"I swear, on my job, that I will pay for the present." She crossed her heart with two fingers held together like a salute.

He picked at the lumpy tape on the improperly matched seam. "The paper is cute. I love the little elves."

"Come on, it won't bite you. Don't make me do it."

"I'll do it. In my own time."

She inhaled impatiently and he laughed.

Laughter was good, right?

With one fast motion, Brad tore off the paper and tossed it aside. He started laughing as he stared at the present. "A chemistry set?" he chortled.

"You said you always wanted one. Now you can mix dangerous chemicals and do stupid things. With supervision of course," she added haughtily.

"Does this mean what I think it means?" he asked, all laughter gone from his voice though a smile lingered on his lips and in his eyes.

"Yes. Bradley Scott Putnam, you do not have to quit your job. I'll adapt. I'll learn to trust you to be safe."

"First, my name isn't Bradley Scott, it's Bradley James. Second, if I have you to come home to, I'll be the safest man on the squad. In the province."

Slowly without taking his eyes off her, he set the box on the coffee table and took her hands. "Sage Taylor, I've waited forty-four for this moment." He smiled at her and leaned closer. "I'm going to kiss you." He paused. "This is the last chance for you to stop me."

"Bradley James Putnam, shut up and kiss me." She closed the distance between them at brushed her lips across his. Electric happiness jolted through her body as she threw her arms around his neck to deepen the kiss.

His lips were firm and soft. He tasted of mint and coffee. Briefly she wondered how he managed that just after dinner, then she decided she didn't care. She just wanted to spend the rest of her life kissing him. Reveling in the pure sweet love that flowed between them. They kissed until they were breathless. Finally, Brad eased back. She groaned a protest even as she gasped for air. He was one heck of a kisser.

He pulled her arms from around his neck and held her hands again. "One more thing. Sage Elizabeth Taylor, will you marry me?" He dropped to his knees and pulled a velvet box from his pocket. He flipped it open.

She gasped. "It's beautiful. Is that an emerald?"

"It is. It matches the sweater you were wearing the day we met. I wanted to preserve the day for both of us." He swallowed hard. "I can exchange it if you don't like it."

"I love it. It's beautiful. Put it on me."

"You haven't said yes," he griped, half serious.

"Yes, yes. A thousand times yes. I adore you, Brad. I love you. Even if you are a fire fighter. I will marry you."

"Thank God and Christmas," he declared as he slid the ring onto her finger. It fit perfectly. "Merry Christmas, Sage."

"Merry Christmas, Brad, my love. How did you know my middle name?"

"Easy, I asked your boss. He was happy to share."

"I'll tell him a thing or two about confidentiality," she said, though she was touched that Brad wanted to know everything about her.

"Never mind how I talked to your boss, come here, and give me another one of your sweet kisses. Did you know you taste like sugar cookies?"

She laughed. "Will you still love me when I'm old and fat from eating too many sugar cookies?"

"Sweetheart, I'll help you bake those cookies." He pulled her close for another, longer, deeper kiss.

I hope you loved Brad and Sage's story.

Be sure to watch for the next in this delicious series,

Cappuccino Mugs and Fire Fighter Hugs,

Coming February 21, 2024

https://books2read.com/u/brB7vE

About Katie O'Connor

Best-selling author Katie O'Connor lives in Calgary, Alberta, Canada. She married her high school sweetheart and is living her happily ever after. She is the mother of two grown daughters and is extremely proud of her five grandchildren.

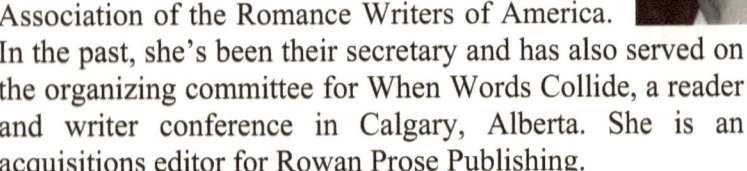

She is the founder of The Write Chicks, a private romance writers' group set up with the sole purpose of supporting each other's writing career. She is the past president of the Calgary Association of the Romance Writers of America. In the past, she's been their secretary and has also served on the organizing committee for When Words Collide, a reader and writer conference in Calgary, Alberta. She is an acquisitions editor for Rowan Prose Publishing.

Katie's career path has been long and twisted, with most of her life devoted to her family. She's been a waitress, chambermaid, cashier, store manager, as well as a lab and X-ray technician. She's been a small business owner and is an avid quilter and crafter.

She's dabbled in writing since high school because something drives her to create stories. She swears it's impossible for her NOT to write. Unsatisfied with one genre, Katie writes sweet small-town contemporary romance, fantasy/paranormal romance, and romantic suspense.

She believes in all things magical, including dragons, fairies, UFOs, ghosts, and house pixies. But most of all she believes in love, romance, and hope.

Where to Find Katie

Website: https://katieohwrites.com
Email: katie@katieohwrites.com
Newsletter Signup: http://eepurl.com/Q2nRr
Facebook: http://www.facebook.com/katieohwrites
Bookbub: https://www.bookbub.com/profile/katie-o-connor
Instagram: https://www.instagram.com/katieohwrites/
Goodreads:
https://www.goodreads.com/author/show/5362469.Katie_O
_Connor

Books by Katie O'Connor

Coyote Creek:
A Lesson in Love 1
A Heart Torn Apart 2
A Secret to Shatter 3
A Melody for Christmas 4
A Surrender so Sweet 5
A Place Called Home 6
A Love to Rebuild 7
Coming Home for Christmas 8
Coyote Creek Box Set 1
Coyote Creek Box Set 2

Cherry Lake Fire Fighters:
Sugar Cookie Kisses
Cappuccino Mugs and Fire Fighter Hugs

A Silver Fox Christmas:
Their Christmas Heart
Their Christmas Love
Their Perfect Christmas
A Silver Fox Christmas Box Set

Hearts Haven:
Running Home
Building Trust
Saving Grace
Heart's Haven Box Set

Three Moon Falls:
Fire Magic
Water Magic

Stand Alone Books:
Carly's Heart
Matchmake Christmas
Cupid's Charm
Gingerbread Dreams
Christmas in Silver Creek
Fake Dating at Half Moon Bay
Sleigh Bells Inn
Hearts in the Spotlight
To a Tea
Bulletproof Heart
Protecting Josie
Rekindled Fire